Champion

Anna Hackett

Champion

Published by Anna Hackett
Copyright 2017 by Anna Hackett
Cover by Melody Simmons of eBookindiecovers
Edits by Tanya Saari

ISBN (eBook): 978-1-925539-17-2
ISBN (paperback): 978-1-925539-18-9

What readers are saying about Anna's Science Fiction Romance

Galactic Gladiators – Most Original Story Universe Winner 2016 – Gravetells

Gladiator – Two-time winner for Best Sci-fi Romance 2016 – Gravetells and Under the Covers

Hell Squad – Amazon Bestselling Science Fiction Romance Series and SFR Galaxy Award for best Post-Apocalypse for Readers who don't like Post-Apocalypse

At Star's End – One of Library Journal's Best E-Original Romances for 2014

Return to Dark Earth – One of Library Journal's Best E-Original Books for 2015 and two-time SFR Galaxy Awards winner

The Phoenix Adventures – SFR Galaxy Award Winner for Most Fun New Series and "Why Isn't This a Movie?" Series

Beneath a Trojan Moon – RWAus Ella Award Winner for Romantic Novella of the Year

Chapter One

With a wild shout, he brought his sword down, slashing through the training dummy.

The emotions inside Blaine Strong were boiling and molten. A second dummy popped up through an opening in the sand of the training arena, and he sliced its belly open, before spinning in a circle, sword raised above his head.

Two more dummies appeared and, using all his strength, Blaine thrust his sword through the closest dummy's stomach, and chopped the arm off the second.

As the final dummy appeared, he leaped into the air and decapitated it with one wild slash. He landed, skidding through the sand, then attacked the damaged dummy again, with violent hits and thrusts of his sword, completely destroying it.

No more dummies sprang out of the ground. He stood there, chest heaving. The anger inside him was like a beast—wild and hungry, and out of control.

In that moment, even though sunshine from the two large suns in the sky warmed his skin, and a brisk breeze ruffled his too-long dark hair, he was back in the bowels of the underground fight ring that had been his life for several months.

Images peppered his head like a movie on fast-forward. All of them were the faces of the people he'd killed.

Blaine sucked in a deep breath, forcing himself back to reality. Even though he was free, the ghosts didn't seem to stop haunting him. He took another deep breath, which just reminded him that a side effect of all the drugs his captors had pumped into him was losing his sense of smell. Right now, he smelled none of the scents of the arena. He hadn't realized how much he'd used the sense until it had been dulled to nothing.

He scanned his surroundings and reminded himself that he was standing in the House of Galen training arena. He stared at the new gladiator recruits training on the sand not far away, and then over the training arena to the walls of the main Kor Magna Arena adjacent. The immense structure was made of a warm, cream stone, and was a mecca for spectators coming to watch the alien gladiators fight. But unlike the hell of the underground fight rings, no one battled to the death there.

He flicked his gaze to the right, and contemplated the tips of the glitzy buildings in the District. It made him think of a long-ago trip to Las Vegas when he'd been younger. The desert planet of Carthago and the city of Kor Magna offered all kinds of spectacles and entertainment.

Blaine shook his head. He was a long way from Earth and his old life. His previous job had been as a space marine-turned-security specialist for the Fortuna Space Station orbiting Jupiter. But that was all long gone.

He'd been abducted by Thraxian slavers, and after months of captivity, sold into the fight rings run by the Srinar aliens. Forced to fight and kill.

He pulled in a shuddering breath, unable to rid himself of the drowning sensation dragging at him.

Then he heard a laugh—full-throated and feminine.

He looked up, his gaze zeroing in on the long, tall form of Saff Essikani.

The female gladiator was walking into the training arena, her back straight, and her muscled, athletic body clad in dark leather. Her leather top hugged her slim torso lovingly, and left her muscular arms bare. Her long, black hair was in tiny braids that she'd caught back at the base of her neck, and her skin was dark and glossy.

Blaine heard his heart beat like a drum in his ears. It was clear she was strong and an experienced fighter, but he also spotted small touches of femininity. The elegant tilt of her dark eyes, unbelievably long eyelashes, and her long, slender neck.

It took him a second to realize she wasn't alone. Harper Adams strode beside her. Harper had been Blaine's fellow security specialist on the space station. She'd been the first to be rescued and taken in by the gladiators of the House of Galen. In turn, she'd helped to rescue several other human women who'd also been abducted. He wondered if there were any others they didn't know about, out there, somewhere, suffering.

Anger threatened, nipping at the edges of his consciousness. To fight it back, he focused on Saff.

She was tossing a small device up and down on her palm. He knew the egg-shaped item was a net. When thrown, it exploded outward, entangling an enemy. She held a sword in her other hand. Harper was holding two swords, swinging them through the air and smiling.

The women found a spot on the sand, and then began to spar.

Every thought of captivity disintegrated. The women moved with a power and grace that was impossible to ignore.

Blaine had sparred with Harper quite a few times, and trained alongside her on the space station. She was an athletic woman, who used her power and speed to her advantage.

But Saff's style was very different. She was taller, but slightly leaner than Harper, the long lines of her muscular body graceful and elegant. Every time she leaped into the air, leading with her sword, the tiny black braids flew out behind her. He couldn't help but picture her as a warrior queen.

He watched the women move across the sand, swords spinning and crashing, shouting and laughing at each other. They were both working up a sweat, but he could tell this wasn't a fight where there was supposed to be a winner.

Finally, they broke apart. Saff slung an arm

around Harper's shoulders, smiling. Then Harper spotted something across the arena and straightened. She waved to Saff and headed over toward a huge, tattooed gladiator who'd just arrived. Raiden Tiago, Champion of the Kor Magna Arena.

Blaine had been shocked to discover that many of the female human survivors had fallen in love with some of the alien gladiators who'd rescued them. He watched as Raiden—his body covered in intricate black tattoos—wrapped an arm around Harper and pulled her up on her toes to plant a solid kiss on her mouth.

Movement caught Blaine's gaze, and he turned back to see Saff sauntering toward him.

Now he could make out the studded detailing on her leather vest, and better see the way her black leather fighting pants molded to her long legs. She walked like a panther on the prowl.

Blaine felt a rush of heat through his body. It made him stiffen. He hadn't felt much except anger and despair for so long. For the last few months, all his angry emotions had been enhanced and intensified by the drugs the Srinar had pumped him full of before his fights.

To feel this fresh, warm desire for this magnificent woman took his breath away.

"Hey, Earth man. Think you can fight a real gladiator?" She glanced at the destroyed training dummy at his feet, a hint of challenge in her dark eyes.

"Any day," he answered.

A faint smile appeared on her face. "Then let's see what you've got."

He lifted his sword, still getting used to the weight of the new weapon. Saff lifted her own.

Blaine attacked. As his blade met hers, he focused on the fight. She blocked his hit, spun away, and came right back in. She was good.

She fought every day in the arena, and no doubt trained for hours on end. Metal rang on metal, and he saw a few of the new House of Galen recruits stop to watch them. A small crowd gathered around.

"Come on, human," Saff taunted, dancing backward. "You can do better than that."

With a growl, he charged at her. But by the time he swung his sword, she was gone. She ducked down low, and he felt a slice across his fighting leathers on his thigh. Not enough to cut, but enough to leave a deep groove in the material.

Dammit. Gritting his teeth, he attacked again. Emotions flared up inside him, an aggressive anger he couldn't control. Most days, he felt it hammering to get out of him. Before his abduction, he'd been a composed man, in control. If he'd been his usual self, he'd have less trouble fighting Saff.

She came in from the side, and slammed her sword against his. The blow vibrated up his arm and he lost his grip on the hilt. The blade fell in the sand.

The next thing he knew, she knocked into him, and they were rolling through the sand. They ended up with her on top of him, straddling his chest. She laughed, a jubilant sound that rocketed through his body.

"I win, Earth man."

She pinned his arms down. He pushed against her but couldn't move. Damn. She was stronger than she looked.

"Again," he growled.

She looked down at him, studying his face intently. Could she see the ugly blackness that clawed inside him?

"Again," he repeated, shoving the dark thoughts away.

She inclined her head. "Sure. I can beat you all day long."

***

As Saff got to her feet and snatched her sword up off the sand, she felt the anger pumping off Blaine. It pummeled against her empathic abilities and she was glad she'd only inherited a very minor ability to sense emotion in others from her mother.

Ever since they'd rescued him, he'd been fighting this battle inside himself. She'd felt glimpses of his struggles with terrible withdrawals from the drugs the sand-sucking Srinar had used on him. Drugs to pump up his aggression. His first few days at the House of Galen had been spent in agony.

Saff fought back a punch of sympathy, along with the need to skewer any Thraxian or Srinar on her sword. The poor guy had been abducted, pumped full of drugs for months, and forced to fight to the death. He'd been deprived of everything good for a long time.

It was expected that he'd have a little trouble adjusting to his freedom. Especially when the transient wormhole back to his planet was long gone, and he and the other humans were stuck here. She knew Galen was still making Blaine take some therapy sessions with the healers, but it was going to take time.

When she turned around, he was already rushing at her, sword lifted.

Their weapons clashed, and she turned her focus back to the fight. He was human, but he was a big one. She'd gotten used to the women being smaller and not as strong. But Blaine definitely wasn't small or weak, with his powerful body and muscles honed hard by the fight rings. As he wore only a simple strap of leather across his chest, it revealed that there wasn't any fat left on his body anywhere, and also a spill of intriguing dark tattoos over one shoulder.

As his next blow rattled up her arm, she gave herself a mental shake. He was fighting with wild slashes—undisciplined and out of control.

She knew that lack of control bothered him.

Saff danced back a few steps, and discreetly pulled out her net device. As he rushed at her again with a wild roar, she tossed the net. It spun, exploded, and wrapped around his legs, sending him down like a slain *gorgo* beast.

He fought against the net, growling and cursing. She neared him, his emotions slammed into her like a rival gladiator, and she gritted her teeth. She realized he'd lost some sense of reality. He was no longer in the training arena, but fighting like the net was a fight ring killer out to take him down.

Drak. Saff leaped on top of him, pinning him beneath her. She pulled out her knife from the sheath strapped to her thigh, and slashed the net open.

"Easy." She reached down and pressed her palms to his face. "Easy, Blaine."

Dark eyes locked on hers. The torment in them made her throat close.

"Easy, Earth man. I'm here. Listen to my voice." She dug her legs into his side, feeling that heaving chest beneath her body, and grabbed his arms. All that hard strength and power. She ignored the inconvenient and inappropriate trickle of desire.

Finally, he settled beneath her, those strong muscles slowly relaxing. She felt the wild churn of his emotions calm a little, although the savage look in his eyes never quite went away.

She released his arms. "You're a good, strong fighter, Blaine. But you need to learn to use your rage to your advantage."

He sat up, their faces only a whisper apart. "I don't want the rage. Before the drugs and captivity, I had perfect control."

She nodded. "I know you're still dealing with everything. Give yourself some time."

He just stared at her, a muscle ticking in his jaw.

Saff shook her head. She spent her days

surrounded by tough, stubborn males who were terrible at asking for help. "Give yourself a break, and accept what you can't change."

She saw his gaze flick past her. She turned her head, and saw the three human women they'd rescued, along with him, from the fight rings. Dayna, Mia and Winter were all slowly settling in at the House of Galen.

Dayna was showing off some earrings she'd obviously purchased at the underground markets. The big, bold hoops inlaid with colored stones suited the confident woman. She was letting Winter feel them. Despite the best efforts of the House of Galen healers, they hadn't yet been able to fix Winter's eyes. The Thraxians had used the woman as a test subject during her captivity and blinded her. Despite that, she was smiling as she admired her friend's new jewelry.

"They're adjusting," Saff said quietly. "And in time, so will you."

"The Srinar...they changed me." He hesitated, as though the words were caught in his throat. "They forced me to fight, and now I'm...different."

Yes, he was. And if he kept trying to get back to the way he'd been before, he'd just keep being disappointed. But something told Saff that Blaine needed time to accept that.

"Come on, Earth man. I'll buy you a drink."

She jumped to her feet, holding her hand down to him. Just as she had in that fight ring when she'd rescued him.

Reluctantly, he slapped his hand in hers and

allowed her to pull him up.

Then she cocked one hip, wanting to distract him. "Race you to the drinks table. First one there is the winner."

She saw him tense, but she didn't wait for him to respond. With a laugh, Saff spun and sprinted across the sand. A second later, she sensed him racing after her.

Chapter Two

Blaine beat Saff by an inch, but had to use every ounce of his speed. They sprinted in to where long tables were set up under the arched corridor lining the training arena. There were large carafes of drinks and some snacks set out for the training gladiators.

Saff handed him a long, tall glass of something with a faint orange color. He nursed it, watching her fill another one for herself.

"I won," he said.

She snorted. "That was a tie, Earth man."

Blaine shook his head. "I won by an inch."

She straightened, taking a sip of her drink. "I don't know what an inch is, but I don't think so."

A smile tugged at Blaine's lips, and he blinked at the sensation. The expression felt...rusty from disuse. "Do you always have to win?"

"Well, I don't like losing. I grew up needing to win."

A painful look crossed her face, flashing away so fast he barely caught it. He wondered what had put it there.

"I was trained to win." She sipped her drink again.

Blaine's gaze zeroed in on the long, elegant line of her throat. "How did you end up here?"

She smiled now, and it wasn't pleasant. "Much the same way you did."

His hand tightened on the glass, so tight he expected it to shatter. "I want the Thraxians and the Srinar taken down."

Her face turned serious. "We're working on it. Galen's talking with the other gladiator houses who helped us close down the underground fight rings. The Srinar are in hiding, and the Thraxians are conveniently denying any involvement." Her mouth flattened. "Cowards. But Galen won't stand for it."

"So many of my friends died in the Thraxian attack on my space station." Blaine thought of all the innocent scientists, engineers, and security staff. He thought of his boss and friend Sam.

His gaze moved over to where Dayna, Winter, and Mia were standing. He hadn't known these women—they'd been on a spaceship inbound from Earth to the space station when they were attacked. But he was damned glad they'd been rescued from the fight rings. They were talking with Rory—a former engineer from the station—and Harper, and they were all smiling. At their feet, a small robot dog circled, leaping up on Rory's legs.

After everything they'd been through, they could smile. Even Winter, who'd been blinded by the Thraxians in captivity, was adjusting better than he was. Hearing their laughter warmed his heart.

There was nothing more shocking than learning that your planet, all your friends, and your family were on the other side of the galaxy, and that there was no way back.

"Blaine?"

Saff's voice had gentled, and he dragged in a breath. "I'm fine."

He would be. He'd damn well make sure of it. He'd beaten the hard edge of his withdrawal from the drugs...and he'd beat the lack of control still plaguing him. The dark thoughts and the anger were never far away, always choking him, and waiting for the chance to spring.

At least they'd all been able to send some messages home. Madeline Cochran, the civilian commander of Fortuna Space Station, had been working with a tech genius here in Kor Magna. Using micro-wormholes, she'd managed to get some messages back to Earth. He'd sent one to his sister.

Rhonda was all he had in the way of family. He missed her like hell, but she was happily married, with a wonderful husband and two great kids. She was well-looked-after, and that eased something in him.

Saff brought her glass to her lips to take another sip, when they heard the sound of glass shattering, followed by a heavy thump behind them. They both spun, Blaine instantly recognizing the sound of a body hitting stone. Saff gasped. One of the mid-level gladiators was on the ground, convulsing, his glass in shards beside him.

Blaine frowned and took a step toward the fallen

man, but a second later, another gladiator recruit staggered, coughing and choking. Blaine shoved his untouched glass back on the table.

"What the *drak!*" Saff dropped to her knees beside the first man. Blaine helped the second gladiator to the ground, tipping his head back.

Both men were convulsing, green foam ringing their lips.

"Poison," Saff spat.

"What do we—" Blaine broke off as Saff's eyes rolled back in her head. Her body started to tilt to the side.

He caught her before she fell, and lowered her to the ground.

"Saff!"

"Can't...breathe," she wheezed.

"Stay calm." He laid her out flat, pressing a palm to her forehead. She was burning up. "We need the medics," he shouted. No, that wasn't the right word. "The healers." He heard the sounds of shouts and running footsteps. "And no one touch any of the food or drinks."

Saff made a horrible wheezing sound. He saw the faint smear of green foam on her perfectly shaped lips.

"Saff! You stay with me." Panic skittered through him. She was so vibrant and alive, and to see such a strong fighter taken down by something as insidious and cowardly as poison cut through him. "Look at me. Look at me." The last words were shouted.

Dark brown eyes met his. He saw fear and pain,

but her gaze locked with his, and deep in them, he saw the core of strength that was all Saff. For a burning second, he felt connected to her, like he could actually feel her pain and determination.

The thunder of running steps caught his ear, and a second later, Harper, Raiden, and Regan appeared.

"We need the healers," Blaine told them. He didn't look away from Saff, watching as her body trembled. She was fighting back the convulsions. Brave, strong woman.

Regan nodded. "I'll get the heal—"

A massive explosion rocked the building.

Rocks, sand, and debris rained down from above, and without thinking, Blaine threw his body over Saff's.

What the fuck? There were screams and shouts. The rubble continued to fall, and a larger-sized chunk of rock struck Blaine in the back.

Moments later, the dangerous storm abated, and Blaine lifted his head. He saw Raiden hunched protectively over Harper and Regan. They were straightening, staring all around them at the screaming and moaning people.

"Stay calm," Raiden shouted. "Check the wounded."

Not far away, Blaine saw smoke pouring from the bottom level of the House of Galen. Around them stood dazed gladiators, covered in blood.

Then he heard the rattle of Saff's labored breathing. He leaned down and saw her panicked eyes. He grabbed the fastenings of her vest, flicking them open so she could breathe more easily.

But he knew she needed the healers if she was going to have any chance of survival. He knew Galen spent a lot of money on the Medical center, the tech, and the experienced team that worked for him.

"Where are the healers?" Blaine shouted as he pressed a palm to Saff's cheek.

Raiden looked over, face grim. "The explosion was in Medical." Each word came out like a bullet.

Fuck. Blaine's chest contracted. He pressed a hand to Saff's chest. "She's dying. She needs help now. So do the others who were poisoned."

Suddenly, a big, muscled form came out of the smoke and shadows, black cloak snapping behind him. Galen, Imperator of the House of Galen, was several years older than most of his gladiators, with a rugged face. A jagged scar crossed his left cheek, and a black patch was fitted over his left eye. His right eye was an icy-blue that missed nothing.

"Raiden, go to the House of Rone. They're our closest allies. Tell them we need healers. Now."

Raiden nodded and tugged Harper up beside him. The couple broke into a run.

Galen's icy gaze turned to Blaine, and then dropped to Saff. A muscle ticked in the imperator's jaw. "Keep her alive." He spun to help the others.

Other gladiators were arriving, pulling the injured to safety, and checking wounds.

Saff was heaving in air, her body jerking, although her eyes were still open and glittering.

They were really such a beautiful, velvety brown, and combined with her dark, glossy skin, she was stunning. Such a contrast, this woman. Such a tough, experienced, and competitive gladiator, with almost gentle, elegant lines—all the way from her long neck to her slim legs.

"Stay calm." Blaine wasn't sure if his words were just for her, or himself as well. As he listened to her rattling breath and the pained moans around them, anger exploded in his blood. Before, when he'd worked security, he would've been composed and focused in this sort of situation. He would have known exactly what to do.

But now, he was a mass of anger. All he could do was focus on the woman dying in his arms.

"I want to see you fight." He leaned down so his lips were close to her ear. "You are magnificent and strong. I like that. Too much."

Her dark eyes stayed locked on his, but the green foam on her lips intensified. She was gasping for breath now.

"No, Saff. Stay with me." Helplessness, his constant companion since he'd been abducted, washed over him. He wanted to smash his fist into the wall.

He remembered fighting together with Saff in the underground fight ring to take down a vicious *gordo* beast. He'd worked with her, side by side, and she'd helped free him from that hellhole.

The place had been his never-ending nightmare. He'd been mired in death and killing, and been forced to kill in order to survive.

He'd had enough of death. No more. He wasn't letting Saff die.

But beneath his palm, he felt her chest go still. *No!*

In the next instant, her heart stopped.

Ignoring the risk of poison, Blaine leaned over her and started chest compressions. Then he fused his mouth to hers and breathed.

He forced air into her body, and fought back his rage.

Blaine lost track of time. He just kept breathing and pumping. His mind cleared of everything.

Soon, he felt strong hands trying to yank him away. He fought them off.

"Let the healers do their job, Blaine." Galen's deep voice.

Two healers crouched on the other side of Saff's prone body. They were Hermia, like Galen's healers, but wearing vibrant-purple rope belts around their sand-colored robes. They were from another gladiator house. Both were long and slender, with composed faces of bland features. Their brown hair wasn't long or short, and he knew they were neither male or female, but some sort of genderless species.

The healers put bags down and began pulling out equipment.

One attached something to Saff's chest—a small metallic device that sat on her smooth skin. Colored lights began to blink on the device and the healers murmured quietly to each other.

A second later, one of the healers held a small

vial over Saff's lips, dropping a bright-red liquid into her mouth.

Blaine curled his hands into fists and set them on his knees. *Come on, Saff.* For so long, Blaine hadn't wanted anything, except to survive the next fight. Now, more than anything, he wanted Saff Essikani to live.

Suddenly, she gasped, her back arching.

She pulled in a deep breath, and her chest starting rising and falling normally.

"Shh, Saff, take it easy." He grabbed her arm.

The gladiator flopped back, her eyes open and dazed. "Blaine?" Her voice was a raspy croak. "What...happened?"

"Just relax. Catch your breath."

Beside him, Blaine heard Galen release a long breath. Blaine suddenly realized that his own hands were shaking.

He pressed one flat against her muscled bicep, and the other against her hand.

Slowly, her fingers tangled with his. The helplessness choking him faded.

Nothing mattered right now, except for the fact that Saff was alive.

Chapter Three

Saff tried to sit up, but her head was throbbing, and her mouth was as dry as arena sand. A team of Thraxians seemed to be hammering inside of her skull.

Strong arms wrapped around her and helped her to sit. She looked around, blinking and squinting through the smoke, at the dazed and bloodied gladiators. Chaotic emotions battered at her, and she slammed down on her empathic ability and cut it off. The damage done to the building—to her home—made her stomach turn over.

"I want to help." Her voice came out far breathier than she'd expected.

"You just died." Blaine's voice was a growl. "You need to rest."

She shook her head, ignoring the agony that exploded inside her temples. She turned her head, her gaze snagging with Blaine's dark one. "We need every spare hand." She nodded over to where she saw Raiden and his fight partner, Thorin, helping the injured out onto the sand. The two huge gladiators could be gentle when needed.

Her own fight partner, Kace, was working to shift rubble, the muscles in his lean, toned body

21

flexing. The man had spent his life in the military, and he looked calm and centered in the middle of the crisis. The other high-level gladiators, Lore and Nero, were also helping. Mountainous Nero lobbed giant rocks away with ease, with the leaner, more charming Lore working beside him. Just beyond them, Saff saw the Earth women, Rory, Regan, and Madeline, carrying drinks and wet cloths back and forth to the wounded.

Who would dare attack the House of Galen like this? They had to know that Galen wouldn't stand for it and would retaliate in a swift and merciless way.

She looked again at where the smoke was pouring out of the arched windows. Her stomach cramped when she realized the location. "They attacked *Medical?*"

Blaine gave a sharp nod.

It went against every unwritten rule of Kor Magna. Healers were considered off-limits. Non-combatants.

Through the billowing smoke, she saw the dark shape of Galen emerge.

He was pointing and shouting at some gladiators. Saff's chest went tight. She'd seen Galen relaxed, composed, and angry. But the icy rage—sharp as a blade—on his scarred face right now was beyond scary. She felt it prickle along her skin like ice crystals.

"Get me up, Earth man."

Blaine muttered under his breath, but she ignored the comparison to a stubborn ass, whatever that was. He helped her to her feet, and it took her a second to find her balance, wobbling there like a newly born daarn bear kit from her homeworld. Drak, she hated feeling weak.

But determination filled her. This was her home. The one she'd claimed for herself. She moved over to help some blood-and-dust-covered recruits, who were struggling to get to their feet. She helped them up, and then moved to shift some rubble. Instantly, large hands were there to help her. As she moved through the destruction, Blaine stuck to her side, following wherever she went.

They fell into a routine of helping the injured out onto the sand, and clearing away the rocks. Galen would want everything back in order as quickly as possible. It was one of the most important rules of the arena: don't show any weakness.

After the injured were healed and the repairs started, then it would be time to find who had done this.

A scream echoed faintly through the commotion. Saff froze and lifted her head. She scanned the chaos, but didn't see anything that should be ringing alarm bells. There was so much noise and confusion, maybe she'd imagined that scream.

But then she heard it again, the faint sound reverberating through the House. She turned, staring down a corridor that led into the heart of the House of Galen. She tilted her head and expanded her ability.

"What is it?" Blaine demanded.

"I thought I heard—"

Then the scream came again, louder than before. A feminine scream. And this time, Saff felt a faint stab of someone else's fear. When Blaine's body stiffened, she knew he'd heard it, too.

"Come on." Saff broke into a run.

Blaine cursed, and together they sprinted down the corridor. They turned a corner and Saff strained, trying to hear the noises again. Nausea rose, her body protesting the exertion, but she forced it away.

Another scream and some alien shouting.

Saff and Blaine powered around another corner. Ahead, she saw Dayna, Mia, and Winter struggling with four masked opponents. Whoever the attackers were, they towered over the smaller Earth women.

Dayna was the tallest and fittest of the women, and she was fighting back, throwing hard punches. Saff remembered that the woman had been some sort of law enforcement officer back on Earth. Mia was a spaceship pilot, and while she wasn't big, the petite blonde was swinging and kicking with all her strength.

Winter was backed against a wall behind the women, terror written across her face and throbbing off her.

Blaine let out a growl that raised the hair on the back of Saff's neck. He charged ahead of her, barreling into the fight. Saff followed him.

She landed a hard kick into the gut of one attacker, pushing him over, while Blaine wrestled with another man. The two of them slammed into a wall before hitting the floor and rolling. Saff spun, jamming a sharp blow into the shoulder blades of the third attacker. The fourth man was still fighting with Dayna, but she was clearly outmatched. Her opponent was bigger and stronger, and she was still recovering from her months of captivity.

Saff ducked several blows, and jammed her own fist into her attacker's side. This was where her ability was most useful. Getting hints of what her opponent was feeling—anger, fear, determination, rage—helped her refine her attack. When he stumbled, clouded in fear, she leaped into the air, swung her leg around, and smacked her foot into the man's face.

His head flew back, but he didn't go down.

With an angry roar, he charged her. He grabbed her around the waist, lifting her off her feet. As Saff slammed a hard hit into his back, she heard Dayna cry out. Saff lifted her head and saw that one of the attackers had backhanded Dayna. The woman crumpled, unconscious. A second later, the man grabbed her and tossed her over his shoulder.

Saff fought free, and once again traded blows with her opponent. Then a woman screamed.

Mia had been snatched up, and her attacker was struggling to hold her. Mia kicked and flailed.

But the moment of distraction cost Saff. Her own attacker landed a hard punch to her stomach. Saff slammed backward and hit the wall. Pain flared inside her, the air rushing from her already-sore chest. *Drak*. Lights danced in front of her eyes.

She glanced over and saw that Blaine had his man down, was straddling the man's chest, and pummeling his fists into the attacker's face.

The other two aliens were subduing Dayna and Mia, and were huddled near the adjacent wall. *Drak*. They couldn't let these sand-suckers escape with the women.

"Blaine." Her voice was a hushed rasp, and he was too far lost in the blood-lust of the fight.

Her attacker backed away from Saff and grabbed Winter's arm. The woman screamed.

"Lemons!" Winter yelled. "Lemons."

Saff had no idea what the woman meant. "Let her go," Saff croaked out.

They were in the heart of the House of Galen. These bastards had nowhere to go.

But suddenly, a small explosion rocked the corridor. Blaine's big body hit Saff, taking her to the ground. He braced himself over her as rubble rained down around them.

"Up." She pushed Blaine off her. "Get up."

He rolled off her and she jumped to her feet, ignoring her aches and pains. Something had hit Blaine, and blood covered his face, sliding into his right eye.

There was a gaping hole in the wall.

And the attackers—including the one Blaine had taken down—were gone. And so were the women.

Saff's muscles locked. The attacker had used some sort of explosive, and blown a hole out into the public corridor outside. She stumbled out the hole, searching the corridor beyond, Blaine's big, hot body pressed close behind her.

At this time of the day, the arena tunnels were busy with workers and gladiators going about their business. A few had gathered, staring at the hole and the mess around it.

"The people that came through here," Saff said. "Where did they go?"

A couple of the bystanders pointed down the corridor, but when Saff looked, she didn't see them.

The attackers were gone. She looked up, her gaze slamming into Blaine's enraged one.

Dayna, Mia, and Winter were gone.

***

The meeting in the House of Galen living area was tense.

Blaine watched the angry gladiators pacing back and forth across the room. Raiden's jaw was hard, Thorin kept slamming one of his massive fists into the other, and Lore was tossing a coin up in the air. Every now and then, the coin would burst into flames. Kace leaned against the wall, looking like he was running battle plans through his head, and Nero leaned beside him, deathly still, with the exception of a muscle ticking in the big man's jaw.

Blaine knew the House of Galen had a secret business of rescuing unsuitable gladiators from the arena. They freed slaves, the injured, the weak.

But this was clearly the first time they'd been attacked in the heart of their own House.

Harper, Regan, Rory, and Madeline were huddled together around the table, all nursing mugs of tea. Harper and Rory looked furious, while Madeline had an arm around Regan, whose eyes were red-rimmed from crying. Rory's robot dog, Hero, was curled up in Regan's lap, nuzzling her.

Blaine glanced at Saff. He'd been keeping an eye on her since the attack. She looked fully recovered, but he could tell she was still the tiniest bit shaky. Her balance was a little off. Watching her go down earlier, poison frothing at her mouth, was an image that was going to take him a long time to scrub from his head.

Galen strode into the room, his face looking as though it were made of stone.

Saff stepped forward. "It has to be the Thraxians—"

Galen chopped a hand through the air. "Everybody sit."

For once, no one spoke. They all obeyed the imperator's order, and took seats around the long table. Galen stood at the head of the table, pressing his scarred palms to the surface.

"We have two dead Hermia healers, and several injured." His tone was ruthless and cold. "The ones who are okay have moved what medical equipment survived the blast to temporary quarters. We lost one regen tank."

"How did the attackers get in?" Raiden asked. "How did they get explosives and poison into the House of Galen?"

Galen's mouth firmed into a harder line, if that

was even possible. "We ordered new medical equipment. One container was filled with explosives, while the other shipment carried the four attackers, who laced the food and drinks in the training arena." His gaze moved to Madeline. "I need you to work with the Medical team to replace the regen tank and any other damaged equipment as fast as you can."

The former space station commander nodded. If anyone could create organization out of chaos, and get things done efficiently, it was Madeline.

"We also lost three recruits to the poison, and we have several injured gladiators." Galen thumped a fist on the table. "This will not stand." His icy gaze swept the room. "This attack is on me and mine, and we will retaliate until *everyone* involved is dead."

Blaine had known some scary men before, and he'd seen some terrifying fighters in the underground fight rings, but even he felt an icy shiver as Galen spoke.

"Someone took three women under my protection." Galen looked at Nero. "Nero, what did you find?"

"Nero's from a barbarian world," Saff murmured to Blaine. "They are hunters and Nero can follow a trail that I can't even see. Guy's good, really good."

Nero gave one vicious shake of his head. "Whoever took the women was organized. I tracked them to outside the arena."

Lore cursed. "I was with him. It looks like the attackers had a transport waiting. Nero followed it far longer than I thought possible, but we lost them in the middle of the District."

Galen spun and slammed his fist into the wall. Rock crumbled.

At the table, Regan buried her face in her hands. "Those poor women. They've already been through so much, and we promised them a safe place."

Instantly, Thorin was there, pulling his woman into his arms. She turned and curled into his chest.

Rory stood, rubbing her rounded belly and the child growing there. "The people who took them, were they Thraxian?"

Saff shook her head. "No. There's no way Thraxians could hide their horns. The attackers were masked, wearing black, but they had no horns. Blaine brought one down." She shot him a glance. "Beat him up close and personal."

"Any identifying features?" Raiden asked.

Blaine shook his head. "Nothing. They were big, and in good shape, but that describes most people around here."

Saff was frowning, her fingers tapping against her arm. "Before they were taken, Winter yelled something. Lemons. Does that mean anything to you?"

Harper straightened. "It's a fruit on Earth."

Blaine pushed away from the wall. "Thanks to the Srinar, I can't smell." His anger surged like a wave and he forced it down. "Saff, did the attackers have a scent? A citrus smell, tangy and tart?"

Her eyes widened. "Yes! They did."

Galen moved. "The Hezalon. They have a scent like that."

"Who are they?" Blaine demanded.

Saff's nose wrinkled. "They're mercenaries. They work for whoever pays the most."

"But they are known to do a lot of work for the Thraxians," Galen said darkly.

"So if the Thraxians are behind this, it's retaliation for closing down the fight rings," Blaine said.

"And for rescuing the other humans," Harper said.

"And for beating the House of Thrax again and again in the arena," Raiden added.

"There is no love lost between the House of Galen and the House of Thrax," Galen said. "But this has crossed the line. I *will* bring them down. But for now, we focus on rebuilding Medical and finding Dayna, Mia, and Winter." Galen's voice held a dark promise. "I'll meet with our allied imperators, and send out word that we are looking for the women." He paused. "Someone will need to tell our blue guest that Mia won't be visiting him."

The blue alien had been a captive in the fight rings like Blaine. He'd joined forces with them and escaped...but Blaine knew he'd been a prisoner for a very long time. The powerful alien, covered in tattoos, was having a very hard time adjusting and withdrawing from the drugs, and had to be kept caged. Blaine was aware Mia had been going down to sit with him every day. The blue alien was far calmer in the small woman's presence.

He wasn't going to deal well with her abduction. "I'll tell him."

Galen nodded at Blaine. Then there was a sharp knock at the door, and a house worker entered, head bowed. The man handed a message to Galen before backing out.

The imperator opened the paper. Then he looked up and gave them a sharp smile. "The House of Thrax has issued us a challenge. They want to fight in the arena tomorrow night."

"It's a trap," Thorin's voice was an unhappy rumble.

"Possibly." Galen nodded. "They no doubt want to hit us while they think we're scrambling. But if they want a fight, we'll give them one."

"I want in," Blaine said.

Glances were exchanged, and he curled his hands into fists.

"I owe them. I know they attacked your house, your home, but they destroyed my life." Hot emotion flooded his throat and he fought it down. "They tortured me, they forced me to kill, they pumped me full of drugs. I. Owe. Them."

Galen watched him steadily for a long moment, then the imperator nodded. "You're in." He looked at Saff. "You have a day to get him ready for the arena."

Chapter Four

From the edge of the gym, Saff watched Blaine with his friends. He had an arm around Regan and Rory. Harper and Madeline stood across from him, all of them looking down. She didn't need empathic abilities to sense their pain and sadness.

Saff felt a burst of sympathy. So many people here on Carthago had been torn from their lives, separated from their loved ones, but this little group was so far from home, had suffered so much, but they still kept on going.

She was too far away to hear what Blaine was saying, but whatever he said calmed the women. There were a few smiles, Rory punched a fist playfully into his shoulder, and then they all hugged each other before the women left.

Blaine strode across the gym toward her. Galen spent a lot of money keeping Medical well-outfitted, and he did the same with the House of Galen gym. There were weights for strength training, an indoor fight ring and a large, mat-covered area for sparring practice. Various weapons—swords, nets, daggers, and axes—lined the walls.

"You look better." Blaine came to a stop in front of her.

She nodded. "A good night's sleep works wonders. I've recovered from the poison." She shifted her feet and pulled in a deep breath. She'd never been afraid to give credit where credit was due. "Thank you for keeping me alive yesterday."

His gaze ran over her face, and he nodded. "How's everyone coping after the attack?"

"As best as can be expected." It hurt to have their home, their sanctuary, targeted. "Galen has taken mad to a new level, but he's focused on the rebuilding. They started work this morning."

"That's fast."

"He doesn't mess around." Saff straightened. "Well, I asked you to meet me here so we can start our training for the fight tonight."

He nodded. "I have one thing I need to do first."

"Oh?"

"Visit the blue beast man. He deserves to know why Mia won't be visiting him."

Saff sucked in a breath and fell into step with Blaine. "He isn't going to be pleased."

"Pretty sure that's an understatement."

They walked through several corridors in the House of Galen before they took stairs down to the basement levels. It was darker there, the only light coming from orange lights set into the walls. Saff stared at the heavy-duty cells ahead. Even from a distance, she sensed the black, chaotic emotions pumping out of the cell.

A tall guard nodded at them and they stopped by

a cell with a heavy door with some bars set in the center of it.

Blaine cleared his throat and stepped closer.

Suddenly, the door rattled and Saff had to control the urge to jerk. She saw the huge blue alien staring out at them, gold eyes glowing. His long dark hair fell past his muscled shoulders and faint swirls of tattoos covered his skin. To Saff, he felt like a throbbing mass of rage.

"Hey, Blue," Blaine said.

As far as Saff knew, the alien hadn't spoken. Not even to Mia.

"I've got some bad news—" Blaine drew in a deep breath "—we were attacked here yesterday, and...damn, there is no easy way to tell you this. Mia was taken. Stolen with the other women, Dayna and Winter."

The blue alien went very still and Saff could almost swear she felt the temperature drop.

"We are doing everything to find her and get her back," Blaine added.

The blue alien's hands curled around the bars. "Mi-a."

Blaine stepped closer. "We'll get her back."

"Mi-a." The beast man's voice rose, along with his tumultuous, rage-filled emotions. "Mia!"

The alien exploded into a frenzy, and both Saff and Blaine stepped back. Horrified, she watched the alien tear around his cell, destroying his bunk in a whirl of fists. He slammed kicks and blows against the walls, pulverizing rock into dust.

"Jesus." Blaine just stared.

"Best just to leave him," the guard said. "Poor guy takes a while to come down when he rages." The tall man's eyes were solemn. "Sorry to hear about the women. Mia is really nice. Spends hours sitting outside Blue's cell and even sings to him." The guard shook his head. "Only time the guy sleeps."

Sorrow dragging on her, Saff left with Blaine. As they walked, she felt the tension in him. "This isn't your fault, Blaine."

His jaw tightened. "I don't want to talk, I want to train."

"I'm happy to oblige, Earth man." She wouldn't mind pounding something right now, herself. She led him back to the gym.

He took in the equipment and the mats, and the fighting ring in the corner. "Why not outside, in the training arena?"

"Oh, we'll get there." She walked over to the wall and found what she wanted. The fighting sticks were crafted on the planet Kaan-Tie from *mewa* wood. She held a set out to him. "For now, we'll start with these." She headed out onto the mats.

With one stick, she pointed out the edges of a single mat. "You need to stay in the confines of the mat. You'll need to be aware of your position, and exert some control to keep your body inside the boundaries during the fight."

A muscle ticked in Blaine's jaw. "Control isn't my...strong suit right now."

She tilted her head. "That's okay, Earth man. There are lots of wild gladiators out there in the arena. You've seen Thorin fight. You need to learn to use that lack of control to your advantage. Don't let it use you."

Blaine's hands flexed on the fighting sticks. She watched as his knuckles turned white.

"You don't understand. Before...I was always controlled. I *like* control."

And that was eating him up inside. She lowered her voice, aiming to offer reassurance, but *drak*, Saff had never been the soft and soothing sort. "You might never be like you were before, Blaine. And you already know that you can never go home."

He strode a few steps across the mat, turning his back to her. He set his hands on his hips, his body tense.

"Use it, Blaine," she urged him. If he didn't learn to embrace it, he'd never find a place in the arena.

After a deep breath, he turned back and lifted the fighting sticks. "Let's fight."

Okay, so apparently she wasn't very good at this comforting stuff. But she could sure as hell help him hone his fighting skills, and give him a way to exorcize the demons.

After showing him some basic moves, they faced each other across the mat. They started slowly at first, the sound of wood whacking on wood echoing around the room.

Soon, their moves started to speed up, the strength of their hits increasing. Saff narrowed her gaze. Something told her Blaine Strong was never happy unless he was pushing himself, fighting for the win.

She felt perspiration bead on her forehead. She was using all her strength to block his moves. He was strong and fast.

Finally, Blaine stepped back, sticks by his side. "Enough with the training. Let's fight. Best of three."

Saff smiled grimly. Maybe this was the distraction they both needed. "You're on."

He attacked first, rushing in with vicious strength. *Whack*. She lifted her sticks, spinning and dodging. He might be fast and strong, but she was more experienced.

A second later, she tangled his sticks with hers, wrapped her legs around his hips from the side, and brought them crashing to the mats. He lunged up to knock her off him, but she shifted, pressing one of her sticks down into his neck.

"Yield."

He smacked his palms against the mat. "Dammit."

Saff bounded back to her feet. "That's one to me."

Blaine snatched up his fighting sticks and turned. She saw him pushing back his fury, and he crouched in a fighting stance, raising the sticks.

They went again, the two of them dancing across the mat, sticks thwacking against sticks. Saff kept part of her attention on the boundaries. If she stepped out, it was an automatic win for him. She dodged, turned, and then dived in a somersault across the mat. With a growl, he came after her, sticks whirling.

His next charge was so fast, she felt a stick whack against her ribs. With a grunt, she stepped back, and a vicious smile of satisfaction crossed his face.

For a second, Saff didn't care about the fact that she'd stepped outside the ring and the fight went to him. That smile... Pure heat curled in her belly. That smile turned him from hard and dangerous, to something insanely attractive.

"Okay, one point each," she said. "This final match is for the win."

He nodded, then reached behind himself, and grabbed the neck of his shirt in his fist. He jerked it over his head, leaving him clad only in simple fighting trousers.

Saff's mouth went dry. She let her gaze drift over him. She'd known he was solid, but the guy had a heavily-muscled chest and abs honed so hard they didn't look real. Her gaze snagged on every scar that marred his skin—each one with a story to tell of grit and survival. Confusion rocked her over her reaction. She spent all her days training and fighting with half-dressed gladiators. She'd seen lots of sexy male bodies, and she was sure she'd seen men much more gorgeous than Blaine Strong.

But right now, she couldn't for the life of her remember who. She moved her head from side to side and shook her shoulders, trying to work out the tension. She didn't need to be distracted by a man's chest.

Once again, he came at her fast and hard, but this time Saff was ready. She dodged, she blocked, and got in some hits of her own.

Thwack. Thwack. The sounds of the hits were punctuated with their harsh breathing.

Suddenly, Blaine lunged in close. She slammed her stick against his, but his second one hit across her chest. She sucked in a breath and he slid an arm behind her back, bending her backward over his arm. Their chests were pressed together, their sticks caught between them. They stayed there for a long moment, frozen in that embrace.

"I win." Masculine satisfaction in his voice.

"An important rule of the arena is not to get cocky." She whipped her leg out, knocking into his knee. He went down.

Saff rammed her weight into him. His back hit the mats, and he grunted. She landed on top of him, straddling his chest.

She brought her stick down on his neck again. "*I* win."

He shook his head, staring up at her. She expected to feel his anger, but he was smiling.

"How come I can't feel your anger?"

"Can't be too upset with a beautiful woman on top of me." Then he frowned, his gaze zeroing in on her face. "Feel my anger?" His big body stiffened. "You know what I'm feeling."

Saff was used to people distrusting telepathic abilities. "I have slight empathic senses. Inherited them from my mother." When his face went blank and she felt the wash of his angry confusion, she felt a slash of hurt. She pushed it away and started to move off him. "Don't worry, Earth man, I only get a hint."

He gripped her thighs, not letting her move. "You can't read my mind?"

"No. I doubt even a strong telepath could bust through that hard head of yours." He was watching her steadily and she sighed. "I get hints of emotion, that's it. And to be fair, you broadcast your anger with your entire body. I don't need any abilities to guess what you're feeling."

His dark gaze turned considering. "That's why you're so good in the arena, and with the net. Your extra senses help you determine where to attack."

She inclined her head. When she tried to move again, his fingers bit into her skin.

"What am I feeling now?" he murmured.

She felt his strong, bright desire wash over her, felt the echo of it in her blood. She shifted and pushed her stick into his skin, and he didn't even react.

"I prefer pretty boys." Young, energetic, and eager to please.

"Easy boys." Blaine reached up, the fingers of one strong hand circling her neck. It was a hold that Saff never allowed anybody to do. But he wasn't holding her hard, and one fingertip stroked the pulse in her neck. "They can't be much of a challenge."

"They know how to follow orders."

"I'm a man, and one you can't control."

"But one that I beat."

That sexy smile crossed his tough face. *Drak* the man for having such succulent lips. She couldn't drag her gaze off his boldly masculine face.

"Kiss me," he demanded.

"What?" Her heart started a crazy rhythm in her chest. "No."

"Afraid?"

She snorted. "I don't ever let myself feel fear."

His hand slipped from her neck, his fingers tracing down her collarbone. She felt the scrape of calluses, and for some reason found that unbearably sexy.

"There's always something to fear," he murmured.

Saff heard the nightmares buried in his voice and that stabbed at her. "You don't have to be afraid anymore, Blaine."

He moved, catching her off guard. He rolled her beneath him, his big body pushing her into the mats, trapping her. "I think you're afraid of your attraction to me."

She reacted on instinct, slamming her elbow up into his chin. It snapped his head back. She wouldn't be trapped beneath a man. Ever. She'd learned young not to ever let anyone pin her down, or control her, or own her.

He moved, and they rolled across the mat. She got her fist into his gut, and he grunted. He gripped her arms, and they rolled again, wrestling.

As they fought, Saff realized he was being careful not to hurt her. For some reason that made her mad again. She didn't need someone to hold back. She was Saff Essikani, best net fighter in the arena. She rolled again and got on top of Blaine, jamming her knees hard into the sides of his body.

"I'm not afraid," she spat at him.

"Prove it."

With a growl, she leaned down and fused her mouth to his.

For a second, he lay frozen beneath her, then one big hand palmed the back of her head, and he opened his mouth.

His tongue invaded, dueling with hers. Sensation exploded through her, and she fought back a moan. He tasted so good.

Drak. All thoughts rushed out of Saff's head, and pleasure rushed in to fill it.

The kiss deepened, and when Saff tasted blood, she realized she'd bitten his lip. He kissed her like he needed her to live. Needed her to breathe. Like he could find all the answers inside her.

Saff wrenched her mouth away from his and shot to her feet.

She stood there, her chest heaving, and looked down at him. This man who, for the first time ever, left her feeling undone. This man from a planet on the other side of the galaxy, with glorious dark skin and dark eyes filled with nightmares.

"If you want to fight tonight, we need to get back to training." She spun and walked out of the gym, telling herself she wasn't afraid, or a coward...but quite possibly a liar.

***

The two suns of Carthago were setting as Blaine tightened his harness and checked his sword again. Outside the tunnel, he heard the roar of the waiting crowd in the arena.

He blew out a breath. He'd fought hundreds of times, this was no different.

Except it was. This time it wasn't just him and a battle of survival. This time, it was a show watched by thousands and he was fighting as part of a team.

"Hey, we came to wish you luck."

Rory's voice made him turn. She was standing with Regan and Madeline.

"Thanks."

"You'll do great," Regan said with a smile.

He hoped so. He hoped he didn't lose it and put the House of Galen gladiators—put Saff—at risk. He looked past the women to where Saff was chatting with Kace.

"Sooo," Rory drawled, "you and Saff."

When he looked back, Rory was wearing a wide, satisfied smile. "She's training me."

"Is that what they're calling it these days?" Madeline said.

He blinked at his former commander. He was still adjusting to the fact that she was more open and friendly now.

"Blaine," Rory said with exaggerated patience. "The sexual tension crackling between you two is outrageous. Saff is awesome. I couldn't think of a more perfect woman for you."

"The last thing I need right now is a woman." He needed to get back to his normal self, shore up his control.

Regan pressed a small hand to his arm. "You need to not forget to enjoy yourself."

He waved a hand at them. "I have a sister, I don't need any more."

"She's too far away," Rory said. "Bet she'd appreciate us stepping in."

"I have a fight to prepare for."

"Stubborn." Rory shook her head. "You do know that we'll be placing bets on how long it takes for you and Saff to do the nasty."

"Go." He shooed them away. "Now."

They all smiled at him and called out good luck before heading over to talk with the other gladiators.

Moments later, he heard the wail of a siren. Raiden moved up beside him. "Time to fight."

Blaine nodded. He was ready. With the others, he stepped out of the tunnel and into the arena.

Noise thundered around him. The stands were filled to bursting with people, and the spectators were shouting, cheering, and screaming.

Memories hammered at him—of being in the underground fight rings, of the blood, the pain, and of watching the light fading from his opponents' eyes.

He breathed deep, looking up at the big, open arena. At the evening sky above. He tried to remind himself that he was no longer trapped, no longer a prisoner.

But the memories had very sharp claws.

Saff moved up beside him and bumped him with her shoulder. Instantly, it snapped him back to the present.

"Ready?" She was holding a net device in one hand, and her sword in her other. She was also watching him with that deliberate gaze of hers, and he guessed that she'd read his thoughts.

Damn. Blaine wanted her to see him as a man, not a broken, damaged animal. "I'm ready."

Around them, the other House of Galen gladiators stepped onto the sand. Raiden and Harper, looking like a warrior couple. Raiden's skin gleamed from the oil that had been rubbed on it, his tattoos on display. Harper looked like she'd been born with a sword in her hand and fighting leathers on her athletic body.

Thorin was fighting with Kace, who was usually Saff's fight partner. They looked like they should be an odd pair: the huge, wild warrior, and the tall, straight, military-trained man. But Blaine knew that all these gladiators had been fighting together a long time. One look at them on the sand, and you knew they were a tight-knit team that understood each other's styles, strengths and weaknesses. When one had a weakness, the other had a strength to balance it out. That was what made the House of Galen unbeatable in the arena.

Lore and Nero came last. The showman gladiator was already fingering the small pouches on the belt around his lean hips. Blaine had seen the way the man used smoke and fireworks to wow the crowd. His fight partner wore a cloak made of fur tonight, and a beard covering his strong jaw. He stared at the crowd with flinty eyes.

Blaine glanced at the stands, his gaze zeroing in on the House of Galen seats. He spotted Galen's broad form, and the human women beside him. Rory gave a wild wave and a whistle.

But then, the timbre of the crowd changed, the shouts rising. Blaine turned.

Across the sand, the House of Thrax gladiators stepped into the arena.

Blaine would never forget the moment he'd first seen one of the slaver alien race. With the alarms blaring on Fortuna Station, scientists running in fear, he'd raced in to fight, and had seen the first of the demon-like species. Over seven feet tall, orange veins glowing beneath tough, brown skin, and a set of black horns swept back off their heads.

Tonight, all the House of Thrax gladiators were Thraxians. *Good.*

Raiden turned, his gaze sweeping over all of them. "For honor." He looked straight at Blaine. "And freedom."

The House of Galen gladiators all raised their voices to repeat the cry. *And revenge,* Blaine echoed silently.

"Let's go." Raiden lifted his sword.

They all broke into a jog. Blaine kept pace, with Saff on one side and Raiden on the other. They moved smoothly into a straight line, picking up speed. He heard Thorin let out a wild battle cry from the other end of the line.

Ahead of them, the Thraxians did the same, sprinting to meet them.

They slammed into their opponents. Blaine crashed his sword against that of a massive Thraxian.

The sound of fighting filled the air, with the background soundtrack of the cheers of the crowd. Beside Blaine, Saff was whirling like a storm, her sword deadly. Blaine blocked his opponent's swing, then sliced the gladiator across the chest. The alien fell back with a cry. Blaine looked over to see Saff take her rival down. She was fierce, lethal and beautiful.

Energy coursing through him, Blaine took another Thraxian down. He leaped over the fallen body, and landed on the back of another, driving him to the ground.

He let the red haze of the fight overtake him. These were his enemies and he was getting his revenge.

All of a sudden, he heard shouts, and spun. From a tunnel on the other side of the arena, two Thraxians emerged, riding giant, horse-like creatures.

The large animals had skin as thick as the Thraxians, with giant hooves and sharp teeth.

What the hell? They were like horses on steroids, and they had the same glowing orange eyes as their masters. They thundered across the arena toward the House of Galen gladiators.

"Saff! Kace!" Raiden yelled.

Instantly, the two gladiators ran forward. Saff

pulled out her net device, poised with her arm held back. Beside her, her fight partner lifted his combat staff, holding it out.

Both were calm and focused. It was clear they had done this before.

But as the sound of pounding hooves increased, Blaine's pulse spiked. If they screwed this up, Saff and Kace would be trampled.

Saff tossed the net. She aimed it perfectly, and it flew outward, tangling in the front legs of both creatures. As the animals fell, Kace leaped forward. He knocked the riders off with hard, precise hits. He left them out cold beside their disabled creatures.

Blaine grinned. *Impressive as hell.*

He charged in. A Thraxian with an axe was running at him. *Come on, you bastard.* Blaine swung his sword, tightening his grip. He wanted to tear the alien's head off. He wanted to make the alien bleed.

His gaze met the Thraxian's. Eye to eye. Personal.

Blaine let out a roar and tossed his sword aside. He saw the Thraxian's eyes widen, but before the alien could lift his axe, Blaine was on him.

He hammered his fists into the alien's face. The Thraxian went down on his knees and Blaine kept hitting. He wanted to beat the slaver into a bloody pulp.

Everything around him dimmed. There were no other fighters, no shouting crowd, no arena.

Right now, there was just Blaine and one of the species responsible for him losing everything.

Chapter Five

Saff planted her boot in a Thraxian's gut, and yanked her bloody sword back. She didn't stop to watch the man fall. The House of Thrax gladiators were fighting to maim...and if someone accidentally died tonight, she didn't think they'd mind.

Spinning, she saw Blaine had another gladiator on the ground, beating the Thraxian with merciless hits. She spotted movement and saw another of the aliens advancing on Blaine from behind, lifting a giant axe.

Her throat tightened. Blaine was so lost in the fury of the fight that he wasn't aware of the new danger descending.

Drak. Saff started running, sprinting as fast as she could across the sand.

But it didn't take her long to realize she wouldn't be fast enough. "Blaine!"

Still lost in the fight, he didn't hear her shout.

She snatched a net device off her belt, and skidded to a stop. Centering herself, she tossed the net as hard as she could.

The device flew through the air, just as the

Thraxian reached Blaine, aiming his axe for the human's back.

The net exploded, tangling in the Thraxian's face and arms. As the rival gladiator roared, Blaine spun around.

He tackled the Thraxian, knocking the axe out of his hand. Several hard punches and the alien slumped onto the sand.

Blaine rose, fists stained with blood. Saff stepped up beside him, and they turned. More House of Thrax gladiators were running toward them.

She spotted Blaine's sword in the sand, and, with a flick of her boot, she kicked the weapon up. It flew through the air, and Blaine caught it.

"Ready?"

He nodded. "Ready."

They turned shoulder to shoulder, to face the new wave of Thraxians coming in. Sucking in a breath, Saff centered her thoughts, her gaze narrowing to the fight.

They engaged.

Saff swung her sword, grunting with each hit. Blaine moved beside her in a blur of movement and strength.

He was good. They hadn't fought together much, but he moved out of her way when she needed him gone, and when she needed to pull back, he charged forward. They anticipated each other, and they worked together with a fluid ease that felt so drakking good.

"Left," he yelled.

Saff didn't even have to look. Trusting him, she spun and her sword cut down a gladiator.

Soon, all the Thraxians were down, bleeding and writhing on the sand.

Saff straightened, easing her taut muscles, and turned back to check her team.

They were all standing nearby, staring at her and Blaine. Thorin had his arms crossed over his big chest and a scowl on his face, while Raiden had an amused smile on his lips. The others all stood with their weapons held up on their shoulders.

"You could've left some for us," Thorin grumbled.

Saff grinned at her friends. She felt too good with all this energy crackling through her veins. She felt alive and in charge.

This was what she loved about the arena. Here, on the sand, she was a champion, and her old life was just dust beneath her feet.

She glanced over at Blaine, but he was staring down at the closest Thraxian, lying prone on the sand. Blaine crouched beside the alien. "Where are the women?"

The alien looked up and made a gurgling sound.

Blaine reached out and hit the alien hard with his fist. "Where are they?"

The rival gladiator tossed his head back and started laughing—an ugly, wet sound.

Blaine hit him again, and again.

Saff saw the feral intensity on Blaine's face. All control was gone and there was a wildness in his features that was borne in the nightmares of the fight rings.

Raiden stepped forward, reaching out to grab Blaine's shoulder. But the human turned around, and bared his teeth at the gladiator.

"Wait!" Saff knelt beside Blaine. "Blaine?"

"I need to find them," he ground out. He raised his fist again.

"Don't kill him." Saff leaned in closer. "You can't kill him here. It isn't the way of the arena...and you've left the fight rings behind, remember?"

Blaine's fist stayed there, suspended in midair.

"Let me talk to him." Saff curled her hand around Blaine's and gently pushed it down. Then she looked down at the beaten Thraxian.

He relaxed and sneered at her. She whipped her hand out and grabbed the alien's chin. She jerked his head up, reaching out with her senses.

Oh, he was afraid. Of Blaine. "I'll let him loose on you." She kept her voice low. "After the drugs, the fighting, the torture, everything he's been through...you'll deserve what he does to you."

The Thraxian turned his head and spat orange blood onto the sand. "Drak you."

Blaine burst forward with an inhuman growl, slamming his fist into the side of the alien's head.

Now Saff saw the alien's eyes widen just a fraction. She gripped his chin harder. "Tell us where the women are."

"Is he your guard dog?" the Thraxian spat.

She jerked his head at an unnatural angle. The alien let out a pained yelp. "I don't need him in order to hurt you." She leaned closer. "He's just more motivated than me. But not by much."

Blaine made another sound, and pressed a knee to the Thraxian's chest, putting enough pressure on him to make the alien wheeze.

"The women?" Saff asked again.

"Not here," the Thraxian croaked out. "We don't have them."

Blaine made another terrifying sound and leaned forward. The Thraxian's eyes turned panicked.

"Where?" Blaine roared.

"The Srinar have them. The Srinar took them." The man's orange gaze turned wild. "I don't know all the information. They...they were taken to the desert. They were going to cross the Barren Sands."

Crudspawn. Saff cursed. "How?" The Barren Sands were an unforgiving place.

"The...Corsair Caravan, I think."

She kicked the Thraxian away. Blaine stood beside her, his chest heaving. She felt so much emotion radiating off him, and wasn't sure he even knew where he was. She turned to him, pressing her hands against his sweat-slicked skin.

"Blaine?" No response. She smoothed her hands over his chest. "Come back to me, Earth man."

He leaned closer to her, burying his face into her braids. She heard him breathe deep, and knew he was trying to scent her. It was probably for the best he couldn't smell, since she was covered in sweat and blood.

She stroked his arm, her fingers tracing the interesting tattoos on his strong bicep. "We'll get them back, Blaine. That's a promise."

Brown eyes locked with hers. Deep within them, she saw that he wanted to believe, but he'd had his hopes beaten and broken before.

Her hand tightened on him. "I always keep my promises."

***

Blaine followed the other gladiators through the back streets of Kor Magna. The suns were rising, and he felt the prickle of heat on the back of his neck. His sword was safe at his side, and inside, the need to find the women was like a drumbeat.

They had to find them before they were sold off, or hurt, or worse.

He glanced up and saw Saff was watching him steadily.

"So this caravan is well known?" he asked.

She nodded. "It's used by anyone traveling out of Kor Magna and into the desert." She glanced toward the horizon. "It's dangerous out there. The Corsair Caravan is well armed, and well stocked. They offer good protection, and they know the water sources through the desert."

"Where do they go?" Blaine had gotten the impression that there wasn't much on Carthago, outside of Kor Magna.

"There are a couple of desert trading posts." Saff grimaced. "They're pretty rough and lawless. There are also some forts in the desert that are home to the desert warlords."

Lore leaned forward. "And the legendary Zaabha."

Blaine drew his brows together. "What?"

Saff snorted and shook her head. "Drinking tales."

"There have long been rumors of a vicious, wild arena somewhere in the desert," Lore said, his voice taking on a storytelling tone. "A place of myth and legend."

Blaine knew how bad the underground fight rings had been, right here beneath the city. How bad would an arena be out in the desert? Where even the thin veneer of civilization gave way to nothing?

"We're here," Galen said.

Ahead, the imperator moved under a huge arch of cream stone. Inside was a stone courtyard, ringed by stables. All kinds of alien beasts were poking their heads out over wooden doors, watching them with curiosity.

A man stepped forward to talk to Galen. He was huge, with bulging muscles and legs like tree trunks, but his posture was stooped, and he had a significant limp. If Blaine had to guess, he'd say the man was a former gladiator.

"Galen!" The man clapped a hand on Galen's back. "Welcome, old friend."

"Hello, Varus," Galen answered with a faint smile. "How are you?"

"Good. Good. Being a stable master is a lucrative trade." The older man's eyes clouded for a second. "Not as good as the arena, of course, but good. I have some excellent animals for you."

"Appreciate it."

"I saw that the House of Galen is fighting the House of Rone tonight." The older man's gaze swept over them all. "Shouldn't you be preparing for the fight?"

"I'm hoping we'll be back in time, with our missing friends. Otherwise, my second team will fight."

Varus huffed. "People pay to see Raiden and his team, my friend."

"Still taking in lost kids?"

Varus grinned at Galen's blatant change of subject. "Yes. And I hear the House of Galen is now giving sanctuary to beautiful women."

Galen grunted.

As Varus laughed, he waved his hand at some nearby stableboys. "I have what you requested." Several young boys hurried forward, leading out some massive beasts.

Blaine blinked. The creatures were huge, each with six legs, and powerful bodies covered in a scale-pattern. They ranged in color from deepest black to dark green. One shook its head, and he noticed a small mane down its long neck. It was like a horse and a giant lizard had mated and had a child.

"We're going to ride those?" Blaine asked.

Saff gripped the reins of the lead animal and swung onto the beast in a graceful, athletic move. She patted the side of the animal's neck, murmuring something. She looked at Blaine. "Problem?"

Blaine had always distrusted horses. He'd always found them big and skittish. These creatures made horses look like poodles.

"Afraid?" Saff asked with a smile.

He sucked in a breath and stomped over to another of the beasts. "No."

As her animal shifted and snorted, Saff patted its neck again. "These are *tarnids*. Excellent for traveling through the desert."

Blaine gripped the reins and pulled himself up. As he settled in the saddle, the beast moved, and let out a loud snuff of air. Blaine let out a small gasp and clenched the reins until his knuckles turned white.

Saff studied him with an amused expression, but remained silent.

"This is your guide," Varus said.

Blaine turned and blinked again. A tiny girl stood between Varus and Galen. The giant men dwarfed her. She was wearing loose trousers and a tunic top, all in desert-beige. She had a green scarf wrapped around her neck, and her brown hair was tied in two dark braids that fell over her shoulders. If she was lucky, she might be twelve.

"That's our guide?" Blaine said incredulously. "How old are you?"

The girl cocked a hip. "Old enough to tell you to mind your own business."

Varus pressed a huge palm to the girl's slim shoulder. "Duna is my best guide. Don't let her age or size fool you. She knows the Carthago sands better than anyone."

"She should be at school," Blaine muttered under his breath.

Saff leaned closer. "Probably. But I'd say she's grown up on her own, out in the desert. Varus is known for collecting strays and giving them a home and food in their bellies. The life she's made for herself here with Varus is no doubt far better than what she had before."

Blaine heard something buried deep in Saff's voice, coated with a sense of admiration for this young girl.

Soon, Duna shimmied up on her own *tarnid*, looking minuscule on the giant animal. But, she handled the beast with ease as she led their group out of Varus' stables. The sound of hooves clicking on stone echoed around them.

The strange gait of the *tarnid* felt odd, but as they moved through the streets, he started to adjust. Still, Blaine knew the way his ass was slamming into the saddle, he was going to feel it tomorrow.

The stables were located at the edge of Kor Magna, and it didn't take them long before they were stepping off the paved roads and onto the desert sand. Quickly, the roads gave way to worn desert tracks, the stone buildings gave way to a flat, rocky expanse with only sand dunes in the distance.

As he stared ahead at the pale-beige desert, the walls of the arena and the glitz of the District seemed light years away.

They rode in pairs, forming a line behind Galen and Duna. Harper and Raiden were ahead of Blaine and Saff, while Kace and Thorin, and Lore and Nero brought up the rear. Soon, Blaine couldn't even pick out any sort of track in the rocky sand, but clearly Duna knew where she was going. How, Blaine wasn't sure. She wasn't using any tech, and he sure as hell couldn't see any landmarks. The girl was happily chatting away to Galen, and apparently didn't need the imperator to respond.

It didn't take long for him to feel the searing heat of the suns. Sweat beaded on his brow and trickled down his spine. In the distance, he saw the faint purple smudge of a rocky mountain range.

"Keep hydrated," Saff said, almost as though she'd read his mind. She pointed to the bladder of water hanging off the side of his saddle. Blaine nodded, lifted the bladder, and put the opening to his lips. He took a large gulp. He saw Duna move ahead of their group, kicking her *tarnid* into a fast, loping gallop. She rode like she'd been born doing it, light and easy on the animal. It made Blaine feel fucking awkward.

"So, what do you know about this Zaabha place?" he asked.

Saff gave him a flat stare. "It's a myth."

"Okay, well, what do the myths say?"

She heaved out a breath, sitting so tall and straight in her saddle. "They say it's an arena carved into the rocks in a secret place in the desert, where the desert beasts call home. The local warlords send in their champions to fight to the death in the bloodiest, roughest battles on Carthago." She glanced at him. "Their champions are usually slaves from far-off lands in the stories."

Blaine's gut curdled. It sounded so much like the underground fight rings he'd escaped.

"It's not real, Blaine." Her voice softened. "No one in Kor Magna has ever found it."

His jaw creaked under the strain of gritting his teeth. "I don't need you to tiptoe around me. I survived the fight rings. I can handle talking about it."

She shot him a long glance before nodding.

Suddenly, the sound of pounding hooves made Blaine's head snap up. He saw Duna galloping back toward them, leaning over the neck of her *tarnid*, her braids flying out behind her.

She pulled up in a spray of sand. "Fresh signs of the caravan ahead. They definitely passed this way, and aren't far ahead. We can catch them."

Galen nodded. "Let's move."

"We'll have to ride hard," Duna said with a glint in her eye.

Blaine swallowed a groan, but turned his thoughts to Dayna, Mia, and Winter. The gladiators all kicked their beasts into action and rode hard.

As their *tarnids* hammered across the desert, Blaine just focused on holding on to the reins. Soon, he was soaked with sweat, and had aches in far too many places for him to count. Beside him, Saff rode like some warrior queen, regal in the saddle.

Duna held up a hand and started to slow. They all followed suit.

"I'll take a look around," Duna said. "It looks like they went off the main caravan route. Everyone take a break."

They stopped, drinking from their bladders, as the girl circled her *tarnid* around, staring at the ground.

She came close to Blaine and glanced his way. "You don't like riding."

It wasn't a question. He looked at his *tarnid*. "Not really. I haven't done much of it. I worked in space before I came here."

The young girl's golden eyes went round. "Space?" She glanced up at the sky and then back at Blaine. "That is so liquid."

He suppressed a smile. "Does that mean good?"

"Any sort of liquid out here is good," Duna replied.

"Yeah, well, it was a pretty good job."

"So how did you end up here?"

A bad taste filled his mouth. He'd just proclaimed he could handle talking about what he'd gone through, and he damn well would. "The Thraxians attacked the space station where I worked. They snatched a bunch of us and brought us here."

The girl's nose wrinkled. "I hate Thraxians. The *tarnids* refuse to let Thraxians ride them." She tilted her head. "Can't you go home?"

Blaine felt Saff watching him, but he kept his

gaze on Duna. "It's too far to go back to Earth. I guess this is my home, now."

Duna gave a decisive nod. "I never had a home."

Blaine felt something move through him. He realized a part of him had been angry that there was no way back. But Duna had nowhere to go back to...what did that do to a little girl?

"But Varus found me, and now I have my own room, a bed, food." Duna grinned. "Good food. And I get to ride Yavi, here, whenever I want to, which is extra liquid."

Blaine kept watching the girl as she leaned far out of the saddle, staring at the ground again. He was sure she'd fall off, but she clung with her legs with ease. A girl who'd had nothing and made something of her young life.

"Out of the mouths of babes," Blaine muttered. His gaze met Saff's. She had a faint smile on her striking face.

"There!" Duna shouted, pointing at a patch of ground that looked the same as everywhere else. She lifted her head, looking into the distance. "They've gone to Harmony."

"Harmony?" Blaine asked.

"The Harmony Oasis," Duna answered. "It's not very big or popular, but some of the caravans use it when they need to." The girl frowned. "Corsair doesn't usually go there."

Unless something was wrong. Blaine heard the unsaid words.

They turned, following Duna across the arid landscape. Before long, some faint shapes appeared in the distance. They looked like large rocks.

Blaine narrowed his eyes. He caught a glimpse of a small pool of water, and realized the lumps of rock surrounding it were actually dome-like houses carved out of stone.

"It's not very big," Raiden said.

"It's bigger than you think," Duna answered. "The houses are mostly underground. They mine for multicolored jewels here. Most of the residents are different folk, touched by too much sun. But for the right amount of coin, they'll offer you food and drink...and information."

They slowed their *tarnids,* and walked slowly into the desert town.

A few people looked up from under their doorways. Blaine noted wary eyes, hardened faces baked by the sun.

"No caravan," Duna murmured, as she led them to a small store that was located closest to the murky oasis pool. A thin man in billowing robes rushed forward, carrying a tray of drinks.

"Welcome, welcome! You look like travelers in need of refreshments."

The gladiators swung down and when Blaine's boots touched the ground, his legs protested taking his weight.

"How much?" Galen asked.

The storekeeper smiled, his tanned face full of wrinkles, and named a price.

Thorin sputtered, but Galen lifted a hand. "That's fine. But I want some information, as well."

Blaine grabbed one of the drinks, guzzling it

back. It was lukewarm and tasted a little salty, but he didn't care.

As Galen moved away with the shop owner, the two of them murmuring quietly, Blaine looked around the small town. That's when he noticed someone stealthily watching them from the shadows of one of the houses.

"Saff," he said quietly.

At his tone, she stiffened and moved closer. He leaned his head down, like they were having an intimate moment. He caught the faint scent of healthy, feminine sweat, and he froze.

It wasn't strong, but he could *smell*.

"What did you see?" she murmured.

For a second, Blaine was distracted, thinking of that scent, and wondering what her skin would taste like if he pressed his lips to the back of her long, graceful neck.

"*Blaine?*"

He shook his head to clear it. "There is a Srinar looking at us from the corner of one of the buildings over there. The one with the bright-white dome."

Saff looked up, her lovely, dark eyes meeting his. Then she slowly turned her head, and lifted her drink.

But it seemed that they weren't casual enough. A second later, the Srinar spun and ran.

"Fuck." Blaine burst into action, Saff by his side. They sprinted after the man. Behind them, Blaine heard the other gladiators cursing and calling out.

Blaine pumped his arms, his boots striking the hard-packed sand. The Srinar was ducking and weaving through the domed houses.

Then Blaine saw the man grip the ledge of one of the houses and pull himself up onto the domed roof. This was one of the larger buildings, with two stories and a small balcony ringing the dome.

Where did the idiot think he was going? Blaine didn't stop to think. He sprinted toward the building, grabbed the ledge with both hands and pulled himself up.

"Blaine, wait," Saff yelled.

But Blaine was focused on his quarry. The Srinar started up the curved dome, looking like a spider. Blaine followed him. The smooth rock was slick under his boots, and one of his legs slipped. He pressed his body to the dome and slowed. Any wrong move, and he'd slide right off.

"There's nowhere to go," Blaine shouted. "Where are the women from Earth?"

The Srinar looked at him and spat. The man's ugly, misshapen face had a huge tumor on one side, covering his left eye. Apparently, the Srinar species had suffered a terrible plague and it had set the survivors onto a path of abuse and cruelty.

Blaine climbed higher. He slid his hand down and drew his sword. "I'll ask one more time. Where are the women?"

The Srinar shook his head. "You'll never find them."

Blaine moved upward and watched as the Srinar reached the top. As Blaine got closer, he saw the man hold his arms out at his sides.

Fuck. He was going to jump.

Blaine lunged forward, grabbing the back of the Srinar's shirt. But the man was already pushing off and his momentum dragged Blaine over the edge.

Shit. Time slowed down. Blaine knew he was falling at the wrong angle. If he hit the ground like this, he'd break his neck. Air rushed around him, the Srinar kicking as he fell.

A second later, there was a rush of sound. A net wrapped around Blaine, slowing his fall. It held him for a second, tangled on the railing of the building. Then it let go and he fell the last few meters to the ground, but far slower.

He hit the dirt with an *oof.* Struggling out of the net, Blaine sat up and saw Saff running toward him.

"Are you okay?"

He nodded. "Thanks to you." He got to his feet, dusting himself off, and turned his head.

The Srinar hadn't been as lucky. The man had landed on the sand nearby, his neck and arms twisted at bad angles.

Blaine cursed. "*Goddammit.*"

Then he turned...just as Saff slammed a fist into his belly. The air exploded out of him, and he looked into furious, dark eyes.

Chapter Six

"Are you trying to kill yourself?" Saff wrestled with a vicious surge of anger, and other emotions she refused to name.

Blaine had raced after the Srinar, with no thought to his own safety. He'd nearly broken his drakking neck, and her hands were shaking just remembering. Her hands never shook.

He ran a hand over his head. "No."

"You did a good impression of it." She turned toward the Srinar.

Blaine grabbed her arm. Saff spun and shoved him back a step.

"Saff—"

"You aren't still down there, having to risk your life." The words shot out of her.

He stared at her for a moment. "I know."

"I'm not sure you do." She brushed past him to the downed Srinar. She pressed a hand against the man's neck. He was dead.

Galen and the others appeared. The imperator stared at the Srinar impassively. "The shop owner talked. The Corsair Caravan came through here. They thought they were being followed. They're only an hour ahead of us."

Good. Saff nodded. They could still catch up with them.

"Why was this man spying on us?" Blaine was staring down at the Srinar.

"To warn someone if the House of Galen came in pursuit," Saff said. "But he didn't have the chance."

"As far as we know," Blaine said.

"Nothing we can do now but catch the caravan." Galen strode back toward their *tarnids.* Duna was waiting with the animals. Soon, they were all mounted and heading out of Harmony.

Back in the monotony of the desert, Saff brushed her arm across her face. She really hated it out here in the heat and sand. It certainly made her appreciate the walls of the arena and the comforts she had at the House of Galen.

She purposely didn't look at Blaine.

"I can see something," Duna called out. The girl was standing up in her stirrups, looking ahead.

Saff craned her neck and, for a second, she wasn't sure what she was looking at. All she could see were small mounds on the ground.

Then she realized.

They were bodies.

"Yah!" Duna kicked her beast into a gallop. Galen was right behind her.

Saff rode hard, and soon pulled up beside Galen. She stared at the bodies and a few crates of goods smashed open on the desert floor. "They were ambushed."

Duna nodded. "Sand pirates."

Nice. Saff scanned their surroundings. There

were several bodies and a few dead *tarnids*, as well. Thankfully, she didn't see anyone who looked small enough to be one of the women from Earth.

They all dismounted and started looking around. Saff pulled out her water bladder and took a long drink. The world where she'd grown up had a warm climate but also a lot of water—so the desert wasn't her favorite place.

She hooked the bladder back on her saddle, and patted her *tarnid*s neck. Then she followed along, as the others searched the bodies. She saw Blaine's back was stiff as he checked each corpse. She realized he was still worried one of them could be Dayna, Mia, or Winter.

Saff rolled one body over, staring at the dead pirate. He wore ragtag clothes designed for the desert, and had rough skin, toughened by the desert wind and sun. There were several black scorch marks on his chest.

Sand pirates weren't well organized, and roamed in small bands. They'd steal anything they could get their hands on.

"There are more pirate bodies over here." Duna kicked a mound of sand. "If they have time, the pirates bury their dead facing the setting suns."

"They didn't get the entire caravan," Galen said, his gaze on the horizon. "Corsair can't be much farther ahead."

Saff pulled herself back into the saddle. "But they'll be expecting more company." And if she was in charge of the caravan, she'd shoot first and ask questions later.

They rode hard, leaning low over their *tarnids*. The pounding of hooves echoed in her ears. She glanced at Blaine and saw his face was set in hard lines, his body taut. She frowned at him. He was strung pretty tight—from his ordeal and from his need to find the women. What happened if he broke?

"There!" Thorin called out.

The man had very good eyesight, and it took a few more seconds before Saff could make out the dark shapes in the shimmering heat ahead.

"Watch out!" Duna screamed.

There was a whistling sound overhead. Saff blinked against the bright suns and saw a flaming arrow shooting through the sky.

Her *tarnid* reared up, and she fought to control it. More fire arrows rained down into the sand around them. She heard the men cursing.

Blaine's *tarnid* sprinted ahead. Galen roared at him, and Saff's heart lodged in her throat as she watched Blaine dodging the arrows and moving ahead of their group. She kicked her beast into a gallop. *Drak him*. She wasn't going to let him get himself killed.

"We aren't sand pirates!" Blaine yelled. "We're a rescue mission. We'll pay for information."

The caravan was in a circular formation, their beasts and transports forming a protective wall. More arrows fired...straight at Blaine.

Quickly, Saff snatched a net device and lobbed it. It exploded in front of the arrows, falling just short of Blaine before his *tarnid* trampled it.

"We're House of Galen!" Saff yelled. "Stand down."

The barrage of arrows cut off. Saff stopped her *tarnid* close to Blaine. Before she slid off, Blaine was there, grabbing her around the waist and lifting her down.

"Do I look like I can't dismount myself?" she asked.

He held her close for a second, smelling of sweat and smoke. "No."

"Then why lift me down?"

"So I can get my hands on you."

Blunt, simple words. Her young boy-toy lovers liked to shower her in nonsense flattery about her beauty, and they always left her rolling her eyes. Blaine's words went straight to her gut.

"I don't want a reckless man intent on getting himself killed."

A muscle ticked in Blaine's jaw. "I...lose control. But I don't want to die."

She was still annoyed with him and shoved him away. The rest of her friends arrived, and together, the House of Galen gladiators found themselves facing an armed group of caravan soldiers. They stood in front of their motley group of vehicles and beasts.

Suddenly, the group parted, and a man strode forward. He had a swagger to go with his well-built body and lean hips. He wore desert clothes of a pale-tan color, and a dark leather belt loaded with weapons around his waist. Leather straps also crossed his chest, holding various knives. Shaggy brown hair, tinted gold by the sunlight, curled around a handsome, rugged face.

The man had desert rogue stamped all over him. As she eyed the weapons, Saff wondered if he'd ever been a gladiator.

"I'm Caravan Master Corsair." His voice was a smooth drawl. "This is my caravan."

Galen stepped forward. "I'm Galen, Imperator of the House of Galen."

The caravan master's golden eyes widened a little. "I've heard of you. Why are you attacking my caravan, Imperator?"

"You attacked *us*," Saff said.

Blaine made a growling sound.

"Easy," Galen said before looking back at the caravan master. "We wish you no harm, Corsair. I received information that someone on your caravan is transporting women. Women who were abducted from my house and who have my protection." Galen's voice was sharp as a blade. "We've come to take them back."

Corsair shook his head. "The only women on this caravan are travelers who've paid their fare. Women who are known to me." A look of distaste flowed across the man's face. "I never allow prisoners to be transported on my caravan."

Saff studied Corsair, and saw Blaine was, too. She got the feeling that the man was telling the truth.

Corsair swept a hand out. "You're welcome to take a look."

"Thank you." Galen jerked his head to Raiden

and Harper. The couple slipped through the vehicles and beasts to meet the travelers. They were back minutes later, Harper looking upset. She shook her head.

"Fucking Thraxians and Srinar." Blaine kicked a boot through the sand. "This was to lead us out here and off the trail."

"Srinar?" Corsair straightened. "We were followed and attacked by sand pirates. They drove us off the main route, and before they died, one pirate mentioned the Srinar."

"What did he say?" Blaine demanded.

Corsair's mouth firmed into a hard line. "I didn't keep him alive long enough to find out more."

"There was a Srinar spy in Harmony," Galen said.

Saff's mind spun as she tried to piece it all together. "They wanted us out of the city." By the stars, she hoped they hadn't sent the women off-world.

"But they also wanted Corsair off the regular caravan route, and for you to follow him," a small voice piped up.

Everyone turned to look at Duna. She was leaning against her *tarnid*.

Galen nodded. "Duna makes a good point." He stared out across the vast desert landscape. "They may have still transported the women into the desert and just sent us in the wrong direction."

Saff followed Galen's gaze. So where had they taken the women?

"Or this is all just a ruse to keep us off the real

trail," Blaine said. "And they're back in Kor Magna."

"We know they aren't with the Corsair Caravan," Galen said. "So, we'll keep looking. You have my thanks, Corsair."

The caravan master inclined his head. "I will keep an eye out for your missing women. If I spot them, I'll get word to the House of Galen."

Galen nodded. "Let's go."

They moved back toward the beasts, and Saff saw Blaine, hands by his sides, staring out across the desert. "Blaine?" Her shoulder brushed his arm.

"If they're out here, it'll be like looking for a grain of sand in a sandstorm." Emotion vibrated in his voice. "God, what are they going through? Do they know we'll come for them?"

"I know it feels like an impossible challenge." Saff gripped his arm. When he pressed a hand over hers, she felt his need for the connection. "Once, freedom looked like that to me."

He glanced down at her. "Who took your freedom, Saff?"

A part of her didn't want to talk about the past. She'd buried it long ago, and never let herself think of it. But for some strange reason it tumbled out of her. "My father."

Blaine sucked in a breath.

"I was born without my freedom. My mother was a concubine in my father's harem. He was an emperor on a distant, backwater planet."

"So you were a princess?"

She snorted. "Hardly. I was a slave. From the time I could walk, I was trained to fight. The abilities I inherited from my mother gave me just enough of an edge that I was earmarked as a fighter early on. My father loved to hold huge and lavish fight exhibitions for his guests. He had hundreds of concubines, and hundreds of children. The perfect pool to choose his fighters from." Her heart felt like a hard knot in her chest. She hadn't thought of her mother, or the man who'd fathered her, in years. Saff looked out across the unforgiving sands, thinking of things she would never understand. "My mother loved him." Unresolved anger chewed through her like burning poison. "Despite him having so many other women, despite him owning her, and despite him putting her child—*their* child—in the arena to fight, she loved him.'"

Saff had never understood the sad, desperate emotion her mother had called love.

"What happened?" Blaine asked, quietly, tangling his fingers with hers.

Saff had never held hands with a man. Most men feared her, were in awe of her, or found her not feminine enough. She looked at the way his blunt, scarred fingers looked against her more slender ones. "My father offered me in marriage to a man three times my age. A despot who ruled a nearby moon. My destiny was to fight or to be a commodity in an alliance to a man I disliked." She looked up at Blaine, and saw the sympathy in his eyes. "I defied my father, and in return, he sold me to the Kor Magna Arena. Sometimes things look bad, impossible even, but you have to believe things will get better and keep moving toward it."

Blaine stared at her for a long moment, then he reached out, his callused fingers brushing over her jaw. "Your strength and courage are astonishing."

For the first time in years, Saff fought back a blush. Suddenly, a wind whipped up from nowhere, tossing her braids around and pricking at her eyes.

"Sandstorm coming in," Galen yelled. "We need to get out of here and back to Kor Magna. Like it or not, we have a fight tonight."

Blaine cursed and Saff squeezed his fingers. "We won't give up on them."

A brusque nod. "Right now, I want to fight in the arena." His hand flexed. "I need to fight."

She watched him turn back to his *tarnid*, a chill running down her spine. She felt the ugly emotion pulsing off him. He wanted to be in the arena to take out his frustration—to hurt and be hurt. And despite what he'd told her, she didn't believe he'd be careful out there.

Saff gripped the reins of her own beast. Fine. If Blaine wouldn't protect himself, she'd do it for him.

***

Blaine hammered his fist into the gel bag dangling from the ceiling of the gym. He kept thinking of Dayna, Mia, and Winter. They had to be terrified. He was well aware he was a big guy, but the women were all so delicate compared to the alien species here.

He kept punching his fists into the gel bag, harder and harder, like he could purge the darkness roaring inside him...

Suddenly, the bag burst, splattering blue gel on the floor.

He heaved in some harsh breaths. That was the third one he'd destroyed since they'd returned from the desert.

He looked up, catching his reflection in the mirror on the gym wall. For a second, he barely recognized himself. His face was twisted with anger, and his bare chest was covered in scars and gleaming with sweat. His black hair was far longer than he'd ever worn it, and he snarled. Blaine was out of control, a shadow of the man he'd once been.

And now he realized he might never be that man again.

His hands curled into fists, his chin hitting his chest.

Movement in the mirror caught his attention, and he lifted his head. Saff stood just behind him.

Strong, tall Saff, who ignited something in his blood. Something else he couldn't control.

"You have word on the women?" he asked.

"Nothing yet." She walked up to him, reaching out to touch his back.

"Then why are you here?" he snapped. The nightmares inside him morphed into a horrid ball of hurt and anger, and it wanted to lash out.

She dropped her hand, her face a blank mask. "I wanted to make sure you were okay."

He spun to face her. "You want to help me? Heal me? Fix me?"

Something ignited in her own gaze. "No. I just want you to know that you aren't alone."

He advanced on her. "I feel alone. I'm the only human man on Carthago, hell, in this part of the galaxy. I feel alone when the urge for the drugs is riding me so hard I want to puke."

Saff backed up a few steps. "Blaine—"

He kept advancing. "I feel alone when I'm a lather of sweat in my bed at night and can't sleep. I feel alone when I can't damn well smell a damn thing. Or when thoughts of those women, who I should've kept safe, crawl through my head."

Saff spread her feet wide. "You don't have to go through it all by yourself."

He stepped forward until his chest was pressed against hers. "I'm alone when I remember the face of every person that I had to kill in the fight rings."

"You aren't a bad man, Blaine. You just had bad things forced on you." She lifted her chin. "You think you're the first person who's been forced to kill people?"

A small voice in Blaine's head reminded him that she'd been forced to fight, too. And she'd been just a child. Saff had her own nightmares.

Right now, his own demons were riding him hard, and they needed a release.

He moved fast, sliding his hands under Saff's arms, and lifting her off her feet. She gasped, and he took several strides until her back hit the stone wall.

He expected her to hit him, but she just watched him with a raised brow. "So what now, Earth man? You going to take a hit? Fight with me?"

"No," he growled. Then he slammed his mouth to hers.

Saff went still for half a second, then her arms wrapped around him and she kissed him back.

The kiss was neither sweet nor gentle. It was exactly what he wanted: hard, fast, with an edge. Fuck, she tasted like caramel, and as her hands dug into his shoulders for leverage, her tongue dueled with his.

She nipped his bottom lip. Hard enough to draw blood. He growled.

"What do you want, Blaine?" she purred.

"Not to be alone."

She moved her mouth across his jaw. "You're not. I'm right here. Tell me what you want."

Her voice was like sin, with just enough challenge in it to keep his blood running hot. "Oblivion."

She made a sound, and then shoved hard against his chest. Blaine stumbled back, and when she hit him again, he fell backward onto the mats.

She was on him in an instant, her strong body straddling him. Her mouth was on his again, hard enough to bruise. Blistering heat shot straight to Blaine's cock, making him so hard it hurt.

He heaved his body upward, and they rolled across the mats. She fought, trying to get back on top. Blaine growled and managed to tear her shirt open. Her breasts were high and firm, with dark nipples that right now were perfect hard points. They rolled again. He managed to pin her beneath him, pressing his hard cock against her.

He pulled back enough to stare hungrily at her breasts. "Can you feel how much I want you, Saff?"

"Yes. It feels hot and hungry."

Her torso was perfectly formed, and as he shifted his hands to cup the sweet curves of her breasts, she took advantage. She bucked hard, and Blaine was once again on his back.

Teeth nipped at his chest and he jerked upward. She moved, her teeth sinking into his flesh.

He grabbed a handful of her braids. She was smiling at him. Little witch. If she liked it rough, she'd get rough.

They wrestled again, and this time, Blaine did some biting of his own—those gorgeous breasts, her hard, flat belly. He pinned her down and ripped her trousers away. Finally, she was naked and spread out just for him. He delved a hand between her strong thighs and she moved shamelessly against him.

"You like that?" he growled, sliding a finger inside her.

"Yes!"

He pumped another finger inside her tight warmth, thumb moving through her folds. Saff didn't have a clit like an Earth woman. He moved his fingers inside her, curling them a little. He took his time, smiling to himself, watching emotions cross her stunning face. Suddenly, her hips bucked upward. *Ah, there's the spot.*

Blaine rolled again and pulled her up over him. He saw a startled look on her face. Then he settled her thighs on either side of his head and he saw faint color in her cheeks.

"I'm going to eat you until you come."

She licked her lips. "I hate a cocky lover."

"Then I'd better put my money where my mouth is." He smiled, his hands sinking into her thighs. "Earth saying. Or maybe I should say put my mouth where my mouth needs to be."

"Yes," she hissed.

"Christ, you're drenched. All for me." He smelled her scent—a sweet, musky scent. He froze. *God*. "I can smell you, Saff."

She gasped. "You can?"

"My sense of smell is returning." He lifted his head and grinned. "I can smell you and it is so good." He put his mouth on her, devouring. She tasted good, too. He licked at her before stabbing his tongue inside to find that secret spot. With each deliberate lick and dip of his tongue, she moved above him.

Her cries filled the room and he needed the sound of them. He needed the taste and feel of her. Right here, everything was perfect.

She was rocking her hips against him, her shoulders back and breasts bobbing gently. With another savage thrust of his tongue, her orgasm hit her. Her thighs tightened on his head and she screamed, the force of her release rocking her body.

Blaine rolled over, until she was sprawled on her back on the mats. His own desire beat inside him, loud and insistent. He'd never seen a more beautiful and wanton sight than a naked and well-pleasured Saff.

But reality crept back in as he watched her. She was smiling, her eyes closed, but there was blood smeared across her collarbone, and faint bruises forming on her skin. Marks in the same shape as his fingers and teeth.

Blaine reared back.

He'd never been rough with a woman. He'd always known he was bigger and stronger, and even during sex, he exerted all his control.

He scrambled to his feet and backed away from her.

Saff rose up on her knees, swiping blood from her mouth. Her brow knitted. "Blaine?"

"I'm a monster." His gaze dropped to the bruises forming on her breasts. "You're covered in blood and bruises."

"I liked it." She held out her hand. "I'm not breakable, and I gave as good as I got. You have a few bruises, too."

He just shook his head.

"Actually, you gave and I enjoyed. I'd very much like to taste you, now."

Blaine's cock jumped, but he took another step backward.

Saff stood, seemingly unconcerned that she was naked. She took a careful step toward him. "Blaine, I loved it. A lot. Didn't you hear me scream your name?"

He tried to process her words, but everything

was swirling inside him, beating hard like a drum, crashing and banging. He felt like he did after a shot of the drugs the Srinar had given him—confused, out of control.

"I didn't want to hurt you," he murmured. "I don't know who I am anymore."

"You are who you choose to be," she said. "And I like you, Blaine, as you are. Even though I know you're struggling to sort things out. I want to fuck you, suck you, kiss you."

It was *so* tempting. The oblivion he wanted was right in front of him. He was so turned on by the image of driving himself inside her body, losing himself inside her.

But just like the fights, he knew he'd wake up and have to deal with the aftermath.

He shook his head. "I'm on edge. I...I don't want to hurt you."

She let out a quiet sigh. "Okay."

"I need to keep training. I need to be ready for the fight." He needed this fight, to hammer this horrible darkness out of his blood.

Suddenly, Saff's face went blank. She clasped her hands in front of her. "About that..."

He frowned at her, "What? I'm fighting. I need it."

"Galen hasn't included you in the fight tonight, Blaine."

"What? Why?"

Saff drew in a deep breath. And in that instant, he knew. "You told him I was out of control."

"It was on my recommendation, yes. Since what

happened in the desert...I can sense you have some stuff to work through before you step back out on the sand."

He let out a vicious curse, betrayal cutting through him like a knife.

"Blaine." She held her hand out to him. "I only want what's best for you. I don't want you to get anyone else killed. I don't want you to kill yourself."

He let out a rage filled-roar, then spun and stomped out.

Chapter Seven

Saff lowered her spear, letting the rumble of the crowd around her echo in her ears.

The House of Galen had won the battle in a hard fight against a good house. The House of Rone was a strong ally of the House of Galen, and always provided a good challenge in the arena.

She tossed her braids over her shoulder and took a breath. She should be humming with energy. Instead, she was worried about Blaine.

He'd avoided her for most of the afternoon, and she hadn't seen him before the fight. She thought back to that moment in the gym, his hard, callused hands on her skin. His clever mouth moving between her legs until she'd shattered.

Drak, the man hadn't just driven her to the edge, he'd catapulted her over it. No man had ever done that before.

She sensed someone come up beside her on the sand and turned her head. It was one of the House of Rone gladiators. Calix was smooth and handsome, not a scar on his sculpted body. He was also a hell of a staff fighter.

"Saff, are you free tonight?" There was a glint in

his eye. "I was thinking a private party."

She and Calix had enjoyed a tussle before. He was a fun, energetic bed partner. But right now, she didn't feel a flicker of interest. "No."

"Do you already have plans?" Calix reached out and touched her shoulder with a gentle skim of fingers. "I can meet you later."

Saff lifted her head and looked toward the stands and the House of Galen seats. Her gaze locked with Blaine's. He was sitting beside Rory, Madeline, and Regan, and was staring at her.

"No," she said to Calix again.

The gladiator followed her gaze. "Ah." With surprise on his face, he dropped his hand. "The great Saff Essikani is taken."

Saff made a scoffing noise. "Run along, Calix."

"Never thought I'd see the day." He shot her a smile and jogged off.

When she looked back at the stands, Blaine was gone. She sighed and followed Raiden and the others back to the showers at the House of Galen. In the open shower room, steam billowed.

She knew that there were many women who envied Saff the chance to watch the House of Galen gladiators strip off their fighting leathers and step naked under the water. But seriously, the men were all like brothers to her. She didn't see the sleek muscles and ripped abs. Well, mostly...

As she let the water pound over her head and wash the sweat away, all she could see was Blaine's hardened body.

"We have a party to get to," Thorin called out

from under the neighboring showerhead. "I'm ready to drink and kiss my woman."

Raiden lifted one arm, soaping down his side. "It's just a small party with the House of Rone."

Harper was under the next shower. "Can't say I feel much like celebrating."

Drak, Saff understood. Any thought of the women or her confrontation with Blaine made her stomach churn.

"At least we don't have to worry about explosions or betrayal," Lore said.

No. The alliance between Magnus Rone, Imperator of the House of Rone, and Galen, was solid.

The party would be a good way for the House of Galen to let off some steam after everything that had happened. Although, most of the men had women now, and Kace had even gotten Rory pregnant. Saff knew her fight partner was feeling extra protective and territorial about his lover. She shook her head. It appeared their wild partying days were now behind them, since the men had all gone and fallen in love.

Love...Saff had seen her mother's version of love. She wanted nothing to do with it.

She flicked the shower off and grabbed a drying cloth. After she'd dried off, she found her outfit left for her by the house staff. She slithered into a clean set of fighting leathers, topped with a black leather halter top decorated with studs. It was one of her favorites.

Together with the others, she headed up to the

living quarters. As soon as she stepped inside, she spotted Madeline bustling to and fro, organizing things for the party. Saff shook her head. The woman was always organizing something. Lore made a beeline for Madeline. He'd gone a long way to easing the woman's tension, and she was starting to relax in her new home.

Saff grabbed a drink, scanning the room. No sign of Blaine.

Soon, the party filled with people. There were several mid-level gladiators, House of Rone guests, and even a few arena flutterers. Saff talked to friends and kept an eye on the crowd.

She spotted Galen—wearing his usual black—standing beside a tall, muscled man. Magnus Rone, the Imperator of the House of Rone. The man cut almost as imposing a figure as Galen. But where Galen was a force of nature, Rone was something very different—he was a cyborg.

His dark hair was shaved short and while he was a little taller than Galen, he was a few years younger. His left arm was made entirely of silver metal and she'd heard rumors that his legs were mechanical as well. When he turned, she saw his strong face—with high cheekbones, well-shaped mouth, and one eye that glowed a neon blue. People eyed Rone with one part fascination and one part fear. Saff always felt cautious around the man since he didn't give off a single emotion she could sense.

Finally, the crowd parted and she saw Blaine. He was nursing what looked like an ale, but even across the room, she felt the tension radiating off him. He was wearing a crisp, white shirt that looked gorgeous on his skin, and black trousers. He stared at her, his eyes stormy, and lifted his drink to take a long swallow. Her gaze fell to his strong throat.

Saff was filled with conflicting emotions. For the first time ever, she wanted to comfort a man, to soothe his pain, and she wasn't even sure how to go about it. And right now, she wasn't even sure he'd welcome it.

Suddenly, a pretty flutterer flitted up to Blaine, leaning in close. The woman wasn't much bigger than an Earth woman, and wore a wispy scrap of pink fabric, and had a fall of blonde-and-blue-streaked hair. He looked down at the woman, and whatever she said made him smile.

Saff felt a kick to her gut. It was a full smile. Not the tiny tweaks of lips she'd gotten from him.

He said something and the flutterer threw her head back and laughed.

Something in Saff snapped. She set her drink down and stomped over to them. "Go."

The flutterer looked startled, then pouted, and opened her mouth—

Saff bared her teeth. "Go. Now."

With a huff, the woman turned and stormed off in a cloud of scented perfume.

Saff glared at Blaine. "I don't play games."

"No, you just went behind my back and got me taken out of the fight."

She leaned in close, pushing against his anger.

He was wearing some sort of woodsy scent that suited him. "To protect you."

"I don't need protection. I'm the champion of the underground fight rings, remember?" His voice was bitter.

"Your head isn't in the right space."

He leaned down, his nose brushing hers. "You calling me crazy? Or just an animal?"

His mouth was a whisper from hers. She felt the heat pumping off him. "Stop the careless risks."

A muscle ticked in his cheek. "I can't regain my control, my discipline. No matter how hard I try. I thought you understood—"

She pressed a palm to his chest, feeling the heat of his skin through his white shirt. "I do. But you're trying to be who you once were, and that man is gone, Blaine. You need to embrace who you are now." His big body vibrated and she saw denial in his dark eyes. "Do you want to find Dayna, Mia, and Winter?"

"Yes. But I need to be who I was before."

"And pretend nothing happened to you?" She lowered her voice, her finger toying with the fastenings on his shirt. "You can do better than this."

The muscle in his jaw ticked. "Maybe I should let loose and really enjoy the party."

Drak, he was so stubborn. She stepped back. "You want to fuck a pretty little flutterer? If that helps, then go for it." She waved a hand. "I'm not wasting my time anymore."

She turned away, but a second later, a big body

crowded in behind hers, forcing her forward. He sank a hand into her braids, hard enough to sting her scalp. Saff checked the urge to jam her elbow back into his gut and take him down.

He maneuvered them out a doorway and onto the balcony, pushing her all the way to the end until they were swallowed by shadows. He didn't seem to notice the view of the sparkling city spread out before them, or the bright sprinkle of stars in the night sky.

He spun her, and tugged her head back. "I want you so much it's driving me over the edge." His voice was guttural.

"So take me."

Torment crossed his face. "I…don't want to hurt you. Before—"

"A few scratches and bruises don't even rate on the injury scale, Blaine. I *liked* what we did in the gym. I wish you'd get that through your thick head."

"I have this…darkness inside me."

Her poor Earth man. "We all do. Everyone in the arena does." She hooked a leg around his hip and leaned forward. She sank her teeth into his chest until he grunted. She liked the wet patch she left on his shirt. "Let it loose. I'll help you deal with it."

With a growl, he leaned down, his breath on her lips.

A discreet cough echoed softly in the darkness. "Sorry to interrupt. I seem to be making a habit of that."

Saff let out a shaky breath and looked over

Blaine's broad shoulder. Galen stood there, hands in his pockets, a cool look on his face.

"I've had word from a contact," the imperator said.

Blaine stiffened and turned, Saff's leg slipping off him. "The women? You have their location?"

"Perhaps." Galen's single pale-blue eye was stormy. "Rillian called me. He's the owner of the Dark Nebula Casino in the District, and an ally. He's well-connected, and knows a lot of people across Kor Magna. He also owns a lot of property."

Galen paused for a second, and Saff knew her imperator well enough to know that what he had to tell them wasn't good.

"G? What's happened?" She gripped Blaine's arm.

"The body of a very small woman was found in one of Rillian's warehouses on the outskirts of the city."

Blaine went stiff. Saff closed her eyes and gripped him tighter. *Oh, no.*

***

Blaine kept all his thoughts and emotions locked down as their group headed toward the outskirts of the city. The gladiators kept a tight formation, Raiden and Galen in the lead. Everyone's hands rested on the hilts of their weapons.

Kor Magna felt like a different place in the darkness. There were lots of people headed into the well-lit streets of the District, but here, it was more industrial. By his guess, they weren't far from Varus' stables. Most of the buildings here were large warehouses, and every now and then, he spotted movements in the shadows.

Why the hell would the Srinar bring the women out here? *God.* A part of Blaine prayed that it wasn't one of *their* women they'd find out here tonight.

"Galen."

A smooth, liquid voice came out of the darkness. A tall man stepped out of the shadows.

He was wearing a dark suit with a snowy-white shirt beneath, and his dark hair brushed his shoulders. Blaine recognized someone at ease with wealth and giving orders, but something about the way the man moved said he was just as comfortable in the shadows.

"Rillian." Galen clasped hands with the man. "Thanks for getting in touch."

The casino owner inclined his head. "I wish it was under better circumstances." Rillian led them toward a huge stone warehouse. A team of black-suited security guards stood nearby, laser pistols holstered at their hips.

As they entered the warehouse, there was no sound, except for their footsteps on the stone floor. Inside, the building was full of neatly stacked boxes and barrels. Stores for the casino, Blaine guessed.

Rillian lifted a hand to some guards, and led the House of Galen team down a row of shelves that almost reached the high roof.

Then the man stopped and stepped back, his

handsome face grim. On the ground between the shelves, Blaine spied a small body splayed facedown on the floor, black hair spilling out around her.

His gut went tight. This was his fault. He should have prevented this. Winter had already been through so damn much. His nails bit into his palms. He should have had better control, and fought harder to stop the women being taken.

"No," Harper murmured weakly from nearby.

Surprisingly, it was the gruff, quiet Nero who pushed past Blaine and knelt beside the body. He touched a large hand gently to the woman's shoulder and turned her over, a terrible look on his face.

Saff moved closer to Blaine, and he grabbed her hand like a lifeline. The breath he hadn't realized he was holding rushed out of him.

It wasn't Winter.

Or Dayna or Mia.

The woman's face was lined with ridges across her forehead, and some matching ones on the bridge of her nose.

Blaine felt a rush of dizziness and Saff leaned into him, a quiet, steady support.

Despite their argument at the party, she was still there for him, and warmth bloomed in his chest. He squeezed her fingers.

"*Drak*." Galen went down on one knee. The woman's tattered dress was torn across her chest. The imperator pushed the fabric aside.

The House of Galen logo had been branded into

the woman's skin.

Galen hissed and rose. He turned and slammed his boot into a nearby barrel. Wood cracked. "This is another taunt."

"This smacks of the House of Thrax and those rats, the Srinar," Rillian said. "They're done trading blows with you in the arena, Galen."

"And they left her here because they knew you'd contact me," Galen said. "You're being dragged into this battle, too."

The casino owner lifted a shoulder. "I was already in it. I abhor what both of them stand for. They are no allies of mine."

"They're out for blood," Raiden said quietly.

"I want to take them down." Galen's voice was icy. "Once and for all."

Rillian nodded, his gaze turning considering. "Every house must agree, if you are going to dismantle the House of Thrax."

"I'll get them to agree," the imperator said darkly. "Even if they're not our allies."

Blaine studied the man's face, feeling a shot of admiration. Something told him if any man could do this, Galen could, with his gladiators at his back.

But Blaine wanted to make sure the most important thing didn't get forgotten. "Finding Dayna, Mia, and Winter is the top priority."

Saff stroked his arm. "We will find them. No matter what it takes." She looked at her boss. "Where do we look next?"

A muscle in Galen's jaw ticked. "None of my

contacts have any more information. The Corsair Caravan was the strongest lead."

"You got intel that they were taken into the desert?" Rillian asked.

Galen nodded. "When we reached the caravan, Corsair didn't have them. He claims he never carries prisoners."

"So I've heard," Rillian confirmed. "But other caravans do. Less scrupulous ones."

Blaine tilted his head, studying the casino owner. "You've thought of something."

Rillian crouched again and grabbed the dead woman's wrist. He turned it over.

Another brand was visible on her skin. A circle with an image of a woman with long, flowing locks inside.

Rillian cursed. When he stood, he shoved his hands in the pockets of his sleek trousers. "The brand of the Gaia Oasis. It's famous for its auction blocks."

Blaine felt his muscles cramp. He knew what was coming. "What do they auction there?"

"Women. The more exotic the better."

Saff shook her head. "Gaia is a bad place. I know it's buried somewhere in the middle of the desert, and I've only ever heard terrible things about it."

"And its black-market auctions," Raiden added.

"You think the women were taken there?" Galen asked.

Rillian nodded. "If they were taken into the desert, there's a good chance."

"And this poor woman was just another way to

keep us away until the women are sold," Galen murmured.

"But she's also given you another clue," Rillian added.

"Her death will not be in vain," Galen said.

"I'll ask around," Rillian said, "but I can tell you that the more beautiful and different the women, the more popular they are on the blocks. The more money that's made."

"Scum," Saff bit out.

Blaine knew she was thinking of her past. Of her father.

"I agree with you," the casino owner said. "If you want to check out the Gaia Oasis, you'll need one thing to get in." His gaze scanned them, his dark eyes flickering silver. "A woman to offer for auction."

Blaine cursed, and the other gladiators did the same. Thorin let out a wild grumble.

Rillian held up a hand. "I know, but that's the reality of the situation. You'll need a woman who'll garner a lot of attention." Silver flowed over his eyes now, like liquid metal, chasing out the black. "Any of your Earth women would fit the bill."

Blaine growled and took a menacing step forward. He sensed the tension in the other gladiators, as well.

Saff slammed an arm across Blaine's chest. "Rillian is just stating the facts. All of you throw some water on it."

Galen gave a single nod. "No one is going to put your women on the auction blocks."

"We all know they've been through enough," Saff continued. "Rory's pregnant, Regan and Madeline aren't trained."

Harper pushed forward, avoiding Raiden as he tried to grab her. "I'll do it."

Blaine had watched Raiden in the arena. The man could plow through a field of opponents and never once show any emotion on his face.

But now the look on his face was fierce.

"No." Saff glanced at Galen before her gaze flicked up to Blaine's.

He knew the second he stared into her eyes what she was going to say. The air rushed out of his chest.

"I'll do it."

Chapter Eight

Saff moved about her room, getting ready for their mission to Gaia.

It was strange not to be pulling her fighting leathers on. Instead, she wore a dress. She wrinkled her nose. Her father had made her wear dresses for special occasions. Long, slinky things she'd hated.

Thank the stars this dress was made of leather, and fit her body without hampering her ability to fight. It was fitted to her hips, the seams dotted with beaten-metal studs, and the skirt fell in a fall of plaited leather. It gave glimpses of her legs as she walked, but didn't constrict her. Her leather shoes had ties that circled her calves.

Most of all, she hated that she'd have no weapons. Her sword and nets would stay behind.

She reached for the final object on her bed. A beaten metal collar.

Saff held it in her hands, horrible memories rising like bony hands around her throat.

"Don't do this."

She didn't turn to face Blaine. She didn't want him to see her face right now. "I have to. For those women, your friends. They're in trouble and they're not as strong as I am. I have to stand up for them." Like she'd wished someone had stood up for her when she was young.

He came to her now, his big body pressing in behind her. His arm slid around her, and cupped her jaw. He tugged her head back until their gazes met.

"Brave, and so fucking noble." His voice was a deep rumble.

He leaned down, his warm lips nipping at her ear. Fire raced through her.

"You fight to protect everyone around you, don't you?" he murmured.

As his lips slid down her neck, she couldn't concentrate on his words. She wanted to forget the horrors of her past. The horrors she knew she'd see at Gaia. "Touch me."

He groaned. "We have to go. The others are waiting."

"Just a little. Something to help get me through."

He made a noise and slid his hand down, cupping her breast through the leather. His fingers slid inside the neckline of the dress, touching her nipple. She pushed into his touch and he moved until his mouth met hers. Saff leaned into him and let him devour her.

The desire was so much better than fear.

She heard moaning and realized it was her. She was rocking against him, her tongue tangling with his. Finally, he drew back, nipping her bottom lip gently, before he turned her to face him.

"You aren't a young girl anymore. You aren't defenseless, and you will never belong to anyone but yourself."

His words, spoken in his deep, strong voice, helped to steady her. She nodded.

He stepped back, a hard, intense look on his face. He slid a hand down to adjust his trousers. She saw the very solid outline of his cock pressing against the leather.

"You drive the last of my control away," he said.

And he didn't like it. Saff was surprised to find that hurt. He wanted her, but he didn't *want* to want her. "Bet you always imagined yourself with some small, sweet woman. Someone that you're always in control around, someone you can easily hold back with." Someone he'd take care of in bed, not someone he'd bite and wrestle with.

Silence was the only answer she needed. But *drak* him, the man was misguided.

Saff lunged fast, knocking Blaine back onto her bed. He bounced once, surprise on his face. She landed on top of him, her knees digging into his hips and her body pressed flush against his straining cock.

"I can handle you, Blaine." She shimmied her hips against him, and watched his lips part. "All of you. You don't have to hold back with me."

He gripped her hips, his fingers tightening on her, something hot and blazing in his gaze.

Then there was a knock at the door.

"Time to go." Raiden's deep voice.

Saff slid off Blaine and stood, forcing herself to focus on her mission. Her friends would have her back. Blaine would have her back. For all his issues, she had no doubt of that.

Blaine stood and she saw he held the collar, his face looking like it was carved from stone. She gave a short nod and he fastened it around her. It felt like it weighed more than the stones of the entire arena.

"You belong to you," he murmured.

In silence, they joined the others.

"We can't all travel into Gaia," Galen said. "Blaine, Lore and Nero will go with Saff. Blaine, you'll act as a seller, Lore and Nero will be your protection."

Blaine nodded.

"The rest of us will stay just outside of Gaia. If you need help, we'll be on standby to provide it." Galen held out a small device. "I had Zhim put together two short-range communicators."

Zhim—the information merchant and tech guru who'd created the technology for them to send messages back to Earth. Blaine had yet to meet the man.

"Comms devices don't work well here on Carthago," Galen said. "Minerals in the sand interfere with the signals, but you should be able to get a message through." He handed one to Lore and one to Blaine. "Keep it hidden where no one can find it. You might be searched."

When they left the living quarters, she spotted Regan, Rory, and Madeline waiting for them.

"Thank you," Madeline said to Saff.

Blaine touched each woman's arm. "We'll bring them home."

Soon, Saff followed Galen and the others back into Kor Magna. They followed the same route leading to Varus' stables. When they entered, the scent of animals hit her, and she spotted young Duna standing by some *tarnids*. The young girl lifted a hand, her face grim.

"You're going to Gaia," Duna said unhappily.

Saff nodded. "We have to find our friends."

"It's a bad place. I should be the one to lead you there—"

"I said no," Varus called out. "Girl's been hounding me since I told her."

Saff gripped Duna's shoulder. "We appreciate the offer, but Gaia is no place for a girl."

Duna's mouth moved into a pout. "You'll be careful."

"We will," Blaine said to her.

"We'll even come and visit you when we get back," Saff said. "Or better yet, how about coming to watch a House of Galen fight in the arena?"

Duna's eyes widened. "Really?"

"Sure. You'll be our special guest."

"Liquid," Duna murmured.

The girl helped Varus bring out their *tarnids*. They mounted their beasts and, this time, Saff sat in front of Blaine, like a good little captive, while Nero and Lore had their own animals and flanked them.

"We'll stay back," Galen said as he climbed onto

his *tarnid*. "We don't want to make anyone suspicious."

Saff dragged in a shaky breath and nodded. Blaine wrapped his arm around her waist and kicked their beast into action.

***

Despite the monotony of the trek through the desert, Blaine could feel that Saff was on edge. She kept fidgeting, and even the rocking gait of the *tarnid* didn't seem to lull the tension away.

His gaze fell to the bronze-colored collar on her neck and his anger spiked. That damn thing shouldn't be on that elegant neck. He wanted to rip the offending thing off and toss it in the closest sand dune.

"There's the oasis," Lore said.

Saff stiffened. Blaine lifted his head, and spotted jagged, rocky cliffs rising up from the desert floor in the distance.

As they got closer, he made out the dwellings carved into the rocks. A gap led into a canyon that he presumed housed the main Gaia Oasis. Up on the top of the cliffs, a sprawling, domed fortress clung to the rocks.

Nero was studying the rocks ahead. "Still another hour until we reach the gates of the oasis."

They kept moving, all of them tense and silent. Dark thoughts crept into Blaine's head. What if Dayna, Winter, and Mia weren't there? What if they'd already been sold and shipped off somewhere else on this wretched desert planet? What if they were hurt?

But he forced the thoughts away, and turned his attention to Saff's stiff form. He ran a hand down her arm. "Okay?"

"Yes." A single, determined word.

Ahead, he saw Nero pull his *tarnid* to a halt. The big man's muscled chest was bare, and only crossed by fur-lined leather straps with various knives on them. He tilted his head, looking off into the desert sands.

"What is it?" Lore stopped beside his fight partner and scanned around them.

"I can hear...something." Nero's deep purple eyes scanned the horizon. "Someone's coming. From behind us."

They pulled in closer, and Blaine yanked a spare sword from the saddlebags and handed it to Saff. He looked over his shoulder and spotted the cloud of dust in the distance.

"There!"

Slowly, several battered vehicles became visible through the dust.

"Sand pirates!" Saff yelled.

The four of them leaped off their *tarnids*. The creatures had picked up on the tension, snorting and stomping their hooves. Blaine kept his gaze on the incoming vehicles bumping across the rocky ground. They reminded him of low-riding, military Humvees, but these were beaten up, covered in what looked like salvaged and rusted sheets of metal. Behind them, he saw some other pirates riding *tarnid* beasts covered in makeshift armor.

"I make twenty of them," Blaine said.

"Twenty-one," Nero said.

Either way, they were outnumbered.

Something fired in Blaine's blood. He had to protect Saff, and something in him, something wild borne of the fight rings, reared its head, wanting blood.

Blaine lifted his sword. *Bring it.*

The sand pirates roared closer. "Steady." Nero kept his gaze glued to their incoming enemies.

Suddenly, one smaller vehicle veered off, coming around to flank them. Blaine watched the pirate driving. He was wearing a mishmash of leather, fabric, and even metal as clothes.

On the back of the small vehicle was a strange-looking machine. Blaine frowned. It didn't look like a cannon or any other weapon. What the hell was it? The driver leaned back, the vehicle bouncing, and he flicked something on the machine.

For a second, nothing happened. Then Blaine saw a funnel of wind spin behind the pirate's vehicle. It grew larger, pulling in sand, forming a tornado.

The funnel of wind and sand detached and headed toward Blaine and the others. As it traveled across the desert floor, it picked up more sand, turning into a massive, gritty tornado.

"Sandstorm!" Blaine yelled. "The pirates are generating a sandstorm."

The gladiators cursed and they all braced. Blaine moved closer to Saff. The wall of sand bore down on them.

It slammed into them. The wind blew around Blaine, catching at his hair and clothes. He couldn't see a fucking thing and the sand blasted his skin, stinging.

He realized he couldn't see Saff or the others. "Saff!"

Then he heard the roar of an engine and shouts.

Blaine spun and saw a pirate rushing at him, holding an axe. Nearby, the sandstorm lit up green with what looked like lasers. *Shit.* They had projectile weapons as well.

He heard metal hitting metal. Blaine tried to find that fighting calm he'd once prized, but instead, he felt the all-too-familiar hot rush of bloodlust hit.

Saff was nearby, and he didn't have time to calm himself. He needed to fight.

He embraced the fighting rage and swung his sword. In a whirl, the pirate went down under the storm of Blaine's blows. Another pirate rushed at him, and Blaine slammed his sword against his. As he defeated the next pirate, Blaine knew he needed to find the pirate with the sandstorm machine. He needed to shut the damn thing off.

He tried not to think about Saff. He couldn't see her, could only just make out shadows dancing through the sand. He knew she and the others would be fighting hard.

Blaine pushed forward, searching for any sign of the vehicle. His eyes were streaming and stinging from the sand.

Suddenly, a vehicle gunned past him, almost running him over. He jumped back. It was too large to be the one carrying the storm device. But then he heard the sound of another engine and turned.

He spotted the pirate with the storm device driving toward him at a breakneck pace. The man wore oversized goggles, and sat hunched, leaning forward over the wheel.

When he saw Blaine, he straightened, his eyes going wide, his hand reaching for what Blaine guessed was a weapon.

Blaine raced forward, timed his jump, and leaped into the vehicle.

As he hit the driver, the buggy swerved violently back and forth.

With three hard punches, the pirate slumped beneath Blaine. He grabbed the man and threw him out of the vehicle. Then Blaine searched the unfamiliar controls and spotted a pedal on the floor. He stomped his boot on it, and the vehicle jerked to a jarring halt.

Blaine spun to face the humming machine in the back. When he'd been a cool-headed security agent, he would've taken the time to work out how to switch it off.

But the new Blaine didn't.

This time, he lifted his sword and crashed it down onto the metal with a crunch. He kept up the blows, roaring as he did, and tore the machine apart.

The wind died instantly, the tornado dissipating like it had never existed.

He turned around, and saw Lore taking down a final pirate. No one else was left standing. The other two pirate vehicles had collided, both of them crumpled, their engines smoking.

Blaine leaped out of the vehicle, sprinting back. Where was Saff? He spotted Nero's big form on the ground, half buried by sand.

Skidding to a halt near the gladiator, Blaine pulled the man free of the dune. Lore appeared a second later, helping his fight partner to his feet. The man shook his head, looking dazed. He had a cut to his forehead.

"Saff!" Blaine spun, yelling. "Saff!"

He saw a large pile of pirate bodies nearby. He strode closer and spotted a long, more slender form facedown in the sand.

Blaine's heart stopped. He raced to her, sending sand everywhere as he dropped down beside her. He rolled her over. *Don't be dead.* His heart was beating again, now so hard it hurt. *Please.*

She sat up coughing, her dark lashes coated in sand.

Jesus. Relief flooded him, leaving him a little dizzy. "Okay. You're okay."

She eyed him. "Are you crying?"

He slid an arm around her. "I have sand in my eyes."

She shot him a smile that said she wasn't buying it.

He cupped her chin, leaned down and gave her a quick kiss. "Are you all right?"

She winked at him, shaking her head to clear

the sand from her braids. "Earth man, I took down the most pirates in that fight. I'm feeling perfectly fine."

"I stopped the sandstorm and took down a few pirates as well."

"Pfft." She waved a hand in the air. "Downed opponents are what count."

There was his woman. Competitive steel to the core.

He froze for a second. His woman. His fingers tightened on her.

"Help me up," she said.

They stood and she dusted off her leather dress. The damn thing hugged her toned curves and gave peek-a-boo hints of those sexy thighs of hers.

"Our *tarnids* are long gone," Nero said grumpily.

Blaine looked around, staring at the hot shimmer of the desert around them. No sign of the beasts.

"So, we'll walk," Lore said.

"Hunters do not walk," Nero replied. He strode over to the pirate buggy with the now-disabled storm generator. He tried it and shook his head. "Engine was linked to the generator."

Lore slapped his fight partner on the back. "Looks like you walk today."

"Should we contact Galen?" Blaine asked.

Saff shook her head. "We've lost our transport, but I think we should continue on."

Blaine grabbed Saff's hand, and they turned toward the rocky cliffs of Gaia.

It looked like they were walking to the oasis.

Chapter Nine

Giant metal gates loomed ahead. The oasis was tucked into a canyon, sheer rock walls rising up on either side.

As they entered, Saff saw that the Gaia Oasis was a buzzing hive of activity. Houses and stores were hewn into the rock, and there were people everywhere, most wearing the standard desert robes. Blaine, Lore, and Nero crowded in close to Saff, and she fought back her nerves.

When she saw several women ahead, chained together, she let her nerves morph into anger.

"We all need a drink and a moment to recalibrate," Lore said quietly.

Nero nodded, and pointed at a nearby outdoor tavern. A worn awning flapped in the breeze above some stone tables.

Lore and Nero sank down onto a bench and Nero lifted a hand to order some ales.

Blaine cleared his throat. "Saff, you need to keep up the appearance of being..."

"A slave?" she finished for Blaine.

"I was going to say in character."

As he sat on the bench, she sank to her knees beside his chair. "Don't get used to it, Earth man."

He leaned down, his lips close to her ear. "You on your knees in front of me? I could get used to that."

She tilted her head and lowered her voice. "I'd be happy to do it...under different circumstances."

Heat flared in his eyes.

A server arrived and set their drinks down.

"So, do we contact Galen? Head back to Kor Magna?" Lore lifted his ale.

"No," Blaine said. "We stay. If we leave, the greater the chance we'll lose the women."

Saff nodded. "I agree. We're here now. Let's check out the auctions, find the women, and then worry about finding more transport after."

They all nodded and drank their ales. Blaine let Saff take a few sips from his.

"Time to head to the auction blocks." Blaine pressed a hand to her shoulder.

Saff stood, the collar feeling extra tight around her neck. Blaine held up a small, golden chain. She suppressed a shudder, raised her chin, and pushed her braids off the back of her neck so he could connect the leash to the collar.

She knew the chain was tiny, that she could break it with one good jerk. But it was what it symbolized that made her feel sick.

"I'm here," Blaine said from behind her. "Right beside you, every step of the way."

She gave him a small nod. They headed deeper into the oasis, and the noise of the crowd grew. She saw more and more slave women, many of them naked or near-naked.

They reached a fenced-off area, the doorway flanked by large Thraxian security guards. Saff peered inside at the raised stage ahead—the auction blocks.

A large crowd was gathered inside, and above the noise, she heard other heart-wrenching sounds—women screaming and crying. Her stomach curdled, and she stiffened her spine, choking off her ability. She couldn't afford to drown in the fear and sorrow of these women.

The guards studied Blaine and then Saff. One of them smirked at her, and then waved them in. Nero moved ahead, Blaine beside her, Lore bringing up the rear.

"Lots of Srinar." Blaine's voice carried an edge.

She detested the Srinar. As a species, they'd endured their own pain and suffering in the form of a plague that had left them deformed. But instead of enhancing their feelings of empathy for others, it had left them a species that used and abused.

Blaine and so many others had repeatedly suffered at their hands in the fight rings.

A slim man bumped into Saff, and turned in a whirl of robes that smelled like sweat. "Pretty." He smiled, showing rotten teeth, and reached out a hand to touch her.

Saff slapped him, hard enough for him to yank his arm into his chest with a pained cry.

Blaine jerked her chain. "Behave."

She knew it was just part of the act, but her throat went tight. It seemed the old memories didn't want to leave her alone today. She remembered other men, guests of her father, who'd thought they had the right to touch and pet her like she was a damned animal.

They approached the auction officials. As Blaine talked to the organizers, she blocked out talk of her sale slot and focused on scanning the women near the stage, searching for any sign of Dayna, Mia, and Winter.

Her gaze skimmed the crowd, before landing on the dark-haired woman currently in the center of the stage. She was on her knees, sobbing. She'd been stripped naked, her seller—a large, burly, green-skinned alien—standing beside her watching the bidding crowd dispassionately. People were yelling out bids in a frenzy.

Saff felt everything inside her going as cold as ice. Despite the desert heat on her skin, she felt frozen.

"No," she heard Blaine say firmly.

"It's the rule," the official barked. "I don't make them, just enforce them." He held up a long device.

Saff's stomach did a slow roll. The end of the device was glowing a hot orange. It was a brand.

Blaine shook his head and Saff forced air into her lungs. She held her wrist out.

His gaze caught hers and she begged him silently to let her do this, before she ran off like a coward. He gripped her arm, his body pushing against hers.

The official pressed the brand to her wrist.

The pain was outrageous and Saff gritted her teeth. There was no way she'd cry out. Then it was over and the man stepped back.

She sucked in air, fighting back dizziness and staring at the raw, red mark of a circle with an image of a woman with long, flowing locks inside.

All of a sudden, a warm voice whispered in her ear. "You are freedom. I've never met a woman who belongs to herself as much as you do."

She closed her eyes for a moment. How could Blaine, someone she'd known for such a short time, and someone who'd suffered so much himself, soothe her this easily?

"As soon as we get back, we'll have that healed," he murmured.

She straightened, sending steel into her spine. She could do this. For Dayna, Mia, and Winter. For Blaine. *Drak*, for herself as well, and the girl she'd been. She scanned the crowd, forcing herself to look at the terrified and downtrodden faces of those waiting to be auctioned.

The women were all beautiful, unique in some way. But there was no sign of the Earth women among them.

"Slot T541," the auctioneer called out.

Blaine stiffened. "That's us." He nodded at Lore and Nero. "Move through the crowd. See if you can find them."

Swallowing, Saff looked up at Blaine. After a brief glimpse of serious dark eyes, she dropped her gaze and followed him up onto the stage. Through her lashes, she looked out at the crowd. A sea of interested, excited faces. *Sand-sucking scum.* But a part of her was back in her father's exhibition ring. The crowds baying for blood.

"Just look at me," Blaine whispered so only she could hear.

She did, turning to face him instead of the crowd salivating over her like she was meat.

"This one's a fighter," the auctioneer called out. "Prime fighting stock."

A guard from the side of the stage stepped forward, and before she realized what he intended, he prodded her with the end of his staff.

She spun, reacting on instinct honed in the arena. With a kick to the gut, she made him double over. She yanked the staff from his grip, and, with a hard chop of her hand to the back of his neck, sent him face-planting into the ground.

Blaine tugged on the chain. She spun, baring her teeth, and he snatched the staff out of her hands. "Saff."

She sucked in a lungful of air, and now she heard the whistling and cheering of the crowd. She glanced out and saw many shaking their fists in the air or clapping.

"We have an excellent offer," the auctioneer said.

"How much?" Blaine demanded.

"Twenty-seven binarri coins."

She stifled a gasp. Binarri coins were rare and valuable.

Blaine shook his head. "It's not enough. Auction's over."

The auctioneer's pale face fell. "I can get more—"

"If anyone truly appreciated quality here, you

would have had an offer by now."

The man's face turned sour, but he nodded. Then a man in a hood came up to him and whispered in his ear. The auctioneer turned back to look at Blaine. "The man who placed the bid has invited you to a private negotiation. A few drinks, a chance to meet your merchandise up close, and the opportunity for you to gain a better price."

This could be a good lead. As much as Saff wanted out of here, she also wanted to find the women. This mysterious purchaser could know something.

"Where?" Blaine asked.

"There." The auctioneer stabbed a finger into the sky. Frowning, Saff looked up at the rocky hill looming over the oasis.

The man was pointing at the large fortress carved into the side of the cliff.

***

As they finished climbing the road leading up the hill, Blaine stared at the magnificent fortress. It was made of the same beige rock that was strewn everywhere, and hewn into the side of the cliff. It clung there, lots of curved walls, long, narrow windows and domed roofs. A dominating, ostentatious display of wealth and power.

They reached the large arched doorway that was flanked by two heavily armed guards. The man and the woman stared menacingly at them.

"We were invited here to discuss my slave."

Blaine managed not to choke on the word. Beside him, Saff kept her head bowed.

"Leave your weapons behind, and your guards can wait here, as well." The female guard stepped toward the door. "Bring the woman."

Blaine glanced at Lore and Nero. Their faces said they were clearly not happy at this turn of events. Nero sent an intimidating glare at the two guards that made them both shift uneasily. Blaine reluctantly pulled out his sword and handed it over to Nero.

Finally, Lore nodded. "We'll wait here until you return." His gaze stayed steadily on Blaine's, before quickly glancing at Saff.

Blaine turned, tugging gently on the chain to have Saff follow him. He entered the fortress, his eyes taking a moment to adjust to the dim light.

His eyes widened. Inside, the rock walls were intricately carved with alien scrollwork, and the stone floor was covered in brightly colored rugs. They followed the guard deeper into the palace, through several doorways, and down wide corridors. Then the rooms opened up, and he saw delicate columns and walls made of carved lattice. It reminded Blaine of the Moorish architecture he'd seen in Spain.

They passed a rectangular pool that was filled with large leaves and floating flowers. Across the pool, colored pillows were stacked on the floor, and several women lounged on them. They all wore wisps of jewel-colored fabric, and slave collars around their necks.

Saff walked stiffly ahead of him, staring straight ahead. He looked at the straight line of her spine and wondered if her father's palace had been like this. They moved into another area, and a sleek hunting cat rose from some pillows, staring at them with impassive orange eyes. It had pale fur lined with darker stripes.

Each room they went through was more luxurious than the last. Someone made very good money and lavished it on themselves. The guard stopped at a set of double doors. They were carved of solid stone, and inlaid with a gold-like metal and precious stones. She heaved them open, and gestured them inside.

Blaine stepped into the long room. It was lined with pillars, and far darker than the previous spaces. There was no natural light, just the glow from torches set into the walls.

At the end of the room, he made out the silhouette of a man sitting on a large chair. His face was entirely in shadow.

The guard indicated for them to stop. Saff fell to her knees at Blaine's feet, and bowed her head. Lucky for them she was a damn good actor, and kept her eyes downcast. He knew that one look into her eyes, and any man would see her fierce strength and independence.

"I will pay a good price for the woman." The voice from the shadows was deep and raspy, like the man's throat had been injured.

"She's worth a fortune," Blaine answered.

The man lifted a hand and a young girl scurried

into the room, carrying a tray of drinks. A guard brought a chair in for Blaine. He sat and accepted a glass off the tray. The green drink was frothing, and he sure as hell wasn't putting it anywhere near his lips.

"I'm sure we can agree on a price," the mystery man said.

"I want to trade."

The man went still. "Oh? For what?"

"I like my women small and delicate." Once, that had been true. A lot of his previous girlfriends had been tiny, ultrafeminine women that he'd felt the need to shelter.

He glanced down at the dark head of the woman beside him. Now he knew what it felt like to have a strong woman who fought beside you. It seemed his preferences had changed sharply.

"Really?" the man drawled. "I prefer them spirited."

Something slithered through the man's tone, and Blaine knew that what this man really liked was breaking a strong woman. It left a nasty taste in Blaine's mouth.

"I may have something to suit your taste..." The man steepled his hands in front of him, still little more than a dark shadow. "From your home planet, even."

Blaine stiffened. At his feet, he felt Saff tense as well, coiled like a spring. The sound of hurried footsteps echoed from the hall, and more guards entered the room, swords raised.

Fuck. This man, whoever the hell he was, knew

who they were.

"Quit being a coward and show yourself," Blaine said.

The man rose and stepped forward. He was Srinar, his deep-purple shirt contrasting horribly with the ugly, mottled growths on his face.

And not just any Srinar, but one Blaine knew very well. He was the head of the underground fight rings.

Rage exploded in Blaine. "Bastard." He lunged forward.

Saff leaped up, pressing her body against Blaine's to hold him back. "We're outnumbered."

"He was there. Almost every night." Blaine tried to breathe but his chest was locked tight. "He was the one who ordered the drugs. Always more drugs."

"You are my property, fighter," the Srinar said.

"I belong to no one," Blaine spat.

"You made me a lot of money. Money I've lost since that high-handed imperator Galen interfered." The Srinar tilted his head. "You liked the drugs. I'll have my men bring some in now, and we'll remind you just how much."

"You're a sadistic bastard." Blaine lunged again.

He broke past Saff's hold, but three guards rushed in front of the Srinar, swords held out.

"Where are the women? You took them, didn't you?" Blaine demanded.

The Srinar shrugged. "They are none of your concern."

Blaine turned his head, his gaze meeting Saff's.

She pulled the chain away from him and was threading it in her hands. She gave him a tiny nod.

She wanted to fight. This wild, fierce woman would always stand by his side and help him take down his enemies. Whether those enemies were inside or outside of him.

He gave her a nod back. Like clockwork, they both spun and attacked.

Blaine plowed into the closest guards, ducking swords and smashing fists into jaws. Every time he turned, Saff was there to plug the gap as he regrouped. They worked together, slamming hard blows into the Srinar's guards.

Blaine's blood was singing. He grabbed one guard, gripping the man's harness, and spinning and tossing him. He landed in a nearby fountain with a splash.

Blaine turned and ducked. Tackling one guard and kicking at another. Beside him, he saw Saff shove a guard into a pillar hard enough to crack it.

When Blaine spun again, raising his bleeding fists, all the guards were down and groaning.

"Blaine!"

The urgency in Saff's voice made him spin. She was staring at the empty chair ahead.

The Srinar was gone.

Chapter Ten

Saff saw movement at the doorway. A flash of purple.

"That way!"

She and Blaine bolted out of the room. They raced through the house, following the fleeing Srinar. They broke into a large common area. Saff leaped over some couches, and sent some women scattering with high-pitched screams.

Another glimpse of purple. "There!"

She and Blaine took the corner fast, sprinting hard. They stumbled out into a long corridor. The Srinar was running as fast as he could, but he was no match for trained gladiators.

They gained on him, and Saff dived. She tackled the Srinar, and they hit the ground hard.

"Where are the women?" She got on top of the man, pinning him to the floor.

The Srinar's eyes were wide.

"Where are they?" She slammed his wrists against the floor. She felt Blaine behind her, a big menacing presence. The Srinar's panicked fear battered at her. His gaze flicked past her shoulder. There was no cockiness or confidence now. Only stark fear.

Saff lifted a hand and pressed it to Blaine's chest. He vibrated with the need to attack.

"Tell me," Saff purred, "or I'll let him loose on you."

The Srinar licked his swollen, scarred lips. "I don't have the women. I just dropped the hints that they were here in the desert to lure my champion back."

Drak. Saff stared at him. Was he lying? She couldn't tell.

"If you've hurt them..." Saff's hands itched for a weapon.

"I knew you weren't a slave," the Srinar said. "As soon as I saw you, I knew you'd be perfect for my fight rings."

She stilled. "Galen closed your precious rings."

The man snorted. "Hardly. I just had to move them out of Kor Magna."

Drak, drak, drak. "Where?"

He shook his head violently. "I'll never tell you. You're one of Galen's toys."

"I'm no one's toy, sand-spawn, but that's right, I do stand with Galen."

"That doesn't matter. Everyone can be broken, eventually. Just like him." He jerked his head toward Blaine.

Blaine didn't move, just stared at the man.

"You think he'll ever be whole again?" The Srinar laughed, a harsh, fractured sound. "It doesn't matter where he goes, or how far he runs, his soul is mine."

Without thinking, Saff pulled her hand back and

slammed a punch into the Srinar's head. His head snapped back and he cried out.

"No, his soul is *his*, scum." She punched the Srinar again, opening a gash. Blood started to flow.

"Don't hurt me!" the man whined.

"You have no qualms about hurting anybody else," Saff spat. "People far weaker than you."

"Please—"

"Why should we grant you anything?" Blaine's tone was rough, dark. "Why? I heard others beg you for mercy, and you laughed at them." A harsh breath. "Where did you move the fight rings?"

"I...I closed them down."

"No," Saff said silkily. "You said you moved them, and a man like you wouldn't close down your moneymaker. Where are the fight rings? And where are the women?"

A crazed glow entered the Srinar's eyes. "You'll never find it, and you'll never find them."

Suddenly Blaine lunged past her, slamming a hard fist into the Srinar's face. Blood splattered.

Shouts echoed from deeper in the palace. More guards were on their way.

Drak. They'd be overrun, and they had no weapons. "We need to go. Now!"

Blaine gripped the Srinar's shirt and dragged the man upright, staring him in the face.

Doors burst open at the end of the corridor. Plasma fire splattered the wall beside them.

She knew Blaine was already slipping past rational thought, the wild darkness in him taking over. He wanted answers and revenge, and wouldn't stop until he got them.

She wanted them, too, but it wasn't worth his life.

Saff grabbed Blaine's arm, and yanked him backward. He stumbled with her, dragging the Srinar with him.

"We'll take him with us," Blaine growled.

She wanted to, but he'd slow them down and right now, they needed to get out of there. Already the Srinar leader was dragging his feet and shouting.

"We can't make it out carrying him." She kicked the Srinar away.

Saff yanked Blaine toward a doorway and pulled him through. He let out a low growl.

"Later, Earth man. Right now, about twenty guards are coming after us. Run!"

Thankfully, Blaine didn't argue. They sprinted down a corridor, burst through yet another set of doors, and into another rug-lined hallway. She tried a door, and they slipped inside. It was a well-appointed bedroom, with elegant wall-hangings and a huge, low bed. A large window covered only in elegant lattice looked out onto a large terrace beyond.

"There!" She ran toward the window. Skirting the bed, she picked up speed, turned her shoulder and leaped against the screen. The decorative lattice shattered under the force.

Saff tumbled out, rolling on the tiled terrace before coming back up on her feet. Blaine burst out behind her, landing in a crouch. She stood and assessed their position.

For a fraction of a second, her gaze snagged on the stark, yet magnificent, view of the desert. A flat plain of rocky sand lay in all directions, as far as the eye could see.

"We're on the opposite side of the oasis," she said. "We need to find another way out." She hurried to the railing and looked down.

She cursed. Below them was a sheer cliff, leading down to the desert far below. There was no way down from here. The cliff was too steep and one slip would be certain death.

Beside her, Blaine rammed a fist into the railing.

She spun, looking back along the terrace. They didn't have much longer before the guards found them. Then she spotted something at the end of the terrace, carved into the rock of the cliff. Stairs. "Blaine."

He spotted them and nodded. Together, they ran toward the roughly-cut steps. They appeared to lead up above the house.

As they reached the steps, the sunlight glinted off something on the lowest tread. With a frown, Saff knelt and snatched it up. She held the tiny object out on the palm of her hand.

She sucked in a breath, recognizing it instantly. It was an earring—a hoop encrusted with shiny stones.

"It's Dayna's," Blaine said. "She was here."

The sound of shouts sent them running up the stairs. They came out on a flat platform, and Saff's heart sank.

There was nowhere to go. This platform didn't even have a railing. Beyond it was the steep drop of the cliff and harsh desert below. Behind them were the incoming guards.

They were trapped.

"We fight," Saff said.

Blaine nodded, his face grim.

Suddenly, a loud, earsplitting squawk made them spin. That was when she noticed the tiny overhang in the rock at the back of the platform. Beneath it, a large creature was resting in the shade. It hopped to its feet with a shift of its powerful body. Then, it snapped out its wings.

It was a winged creature the size of a *tarnid*. It wore a thick metal collar around its scaled neck, and a metal chain kept it anchored to the rock.

Saff wasn't sure what the creature was. Carthago's deserts were renowned for its beasts. But looking at it, she felt discordant emotions hit her. It was always harder for her to make sense of what animals felt, but there was one predominant feeling she got from this creature. It wanted to fly.

She glanced at the guards thundering up the stairs toward them, then back at the beast. She hurried over to the creature. "The hook in the wall is old and rusted. We need to break it."

"What?" Blaine stared at the animal. "Shit." But he followed her, grabbed the chain with her, and together they heaved.

They strained again, and a second later, the chain broke free of the rock. Saff took a deep breath, and approached the animal. It flapped its wings, but didn't panic.

"We're going to set you free, big guy." *Drak*, she had no idea how long the thing had been captive. What if it couldn't fly?

With the guards cresting the edge of the platform, she didn't have time to worry. She leaped onto the animal's back. It let out a huge squawk, hopping around on the ground and clearly unhappy.

Blaine jumped on behind her.

Plasma fire spayed the ground, sizzling as it ate into the rock.

Time to go. She gently dug her toes into the creature's side. With another large squawk, the animal leaped into the air, and extended its wings.

Saff let out a wild yell, gripping the beast as hard as she could. Behind her, Blaine wrapped his arms around her waist, his curse swallowed by the rush of air.

The beast dove a short distance, making Saff's stomach dip, before soaring out over the desert.

***

The flap of the creature's wings was loud as they flew through the air. As the animal arced in a wide turn, Blaine tightened his grip on Saff. Fuck, they were a long way up.

He heard Saff laughing as she leaned her body

into the animal's turn. She was *enjoying* this.

But Blaine was acutely aware that they were flying far from the Srinar fortress. *Away* from the Gaia Oasis.

The creature appeared to be heading toward a collection of jagged spikes in the distance. Mountains, maybe? In places, the rocks looked like needles spearing into the sky. He guessed that was the winged animal's home. Blaine sighed. At least it could go home.

He ground his teeth together. The fucking Srinar. They didn't care about any other species. They caught, captured, chained and caged.

And they had Dayna, Mia, and Winter.

He stared up into the pale-blue sky, and then toward the horizon, where the first of Carthago's suns was slowing sinking below the edge. *Hold on. Wherever you are, we'll find you.*

The animal flew higher, catching some thermals and gliding up and down on the hot air. Who knew how long it had been chained, how long it had been deprived of the pleasure of flying?

Soon, they flew in over the strange, twisted mountains. The rocks here were a dark red, and occasionally he saw spiky trees of a brilliant blood-red. Like nothing he'd ever seen before.

Then the creature started to descend. It soared in lower, the rocks getting closer. Blaine spied a winding narrow canyon through the mountains, and the creature headed toward that. As they neared the ground, Blaine's jaw clenched. The damn thing was coming in too fast!

With another flap, it contracted its wings in close to its body. It landed on the rocky ground, skidding a little on the gravelly soil.

Quickly, Saff and Blaine hopped off. The creature spun and snapped at them with sharp teeth. It looked at them for a long moment with intelligent eyes, then with another flap of its wings, it launched itself back into the air.

Shit. As the bird grew smaller in the sky, Blaine realized they were now lost in the desert, far from the oasis, with nothing but the clothes they were wearing.

"Do you still have the comms device?" Saff asked.

Blaine dipped into his pocket and pulled it out. He pressed the button and heard a hiss of static. "Galen? Are you there? Are you picking us up?"

More static.

Dammit. "Galen? Come in, please."

No response.

Blaine's shoulders sagged. "There must be interference or we're out of range."

Saff set her hands on her hips, looking around. She didn't look concerned at all. "We need to find shelter."

"It's not too hot," Blaine said. "We should start walking back to Gaia. Lore and Nero know something went wrong, and will have contacted Galen. They'll be looking for us."

But Saff shook her head. "The suns are setting."

"Right. It'll be cooler."

"Night in the desert brings out all kinds of

creatures. Hunting creatures with sharp teeth. Creatures we do *not* want to run into, especially without our weapons."

Blaine instantly remembered the huge gates of the oasis. He realized they weren't designed to keep people inside…they were for keeping dangers *out*.

"So we need to find shelter." Saff stared up at the steep sides of the canyon "We'll hole up for the night, and walk out tomorrow."

He gave a nod. Together, they headed deeper into the canyon, following the path's twists and turns. The ground was hardpacked, and he wondered if animals used it a lot. Even though the suns were setting, it was still hot, and he felt like the back of his neck was sunburned, his skin damp with sweat.

"Look," Saff said.

He looked to where she was pointing. Up the rocky slope to the side, he spotted the mouth of the cave. He hoped to hell that nothing lived in it.

They scrambled up the slope and entered the darkness. Instantly, the temperature dropped a few degrees, and he savored it. As they moved deeper inside, he realized the cave was actually a tunnel, leading deeper into the hill.

The walls were slick rock in shades of orange, and every now and then small bones crunched underfoot. It didn't look like anything lived here permanently, but it clearly got used for shelter occasionally.

Suddenly, the tunnel opened up into a small cavern.

Saff gasped and Blaine whistled.

The space wasn't big, and was roughly cylindrical. Faint light trickled in from above, and when he glanced up, he saw an opening in the ceiling. But instantly his gaze was drawn back to the rock walls.

"The rock's glowing," he said. The rock pulsed with light, washing the cavern in an orange glow.

Saff nodded. "This type of rock absorbs light from the suns. It'll dissipate during the night."

But that wasn't the only amazing thing. He walked closer to the walls and the alien artwork carved into them.

"Incredible," he said.

"I've never seen anything like them." Saff ran her hand over the pictures. "They look really old."

They made Blaine think of ancient cave art back on Earth. There were simple images of humanoids and animals etched into the stone. People hunting, building shelters, doing activities like collecting water, dancing, burying their dead.

He heard Saff make a sound and he spun. She was standing in front of more art on the other side of the cavern.

He joined her and his jaw tightened. An arena was carved into the wall. It was crude, but the people and animals battling inside it were clear enough.

"The mythical Zaabha?" he asked.

"It could be." Then Saff turned and laughed.

The sound made his head whip around. God, he loved the sound of her laugh.

"Hear that?" she asked.

He tilted his head, and caught the tinkle of water.

Saff grinned, her teeth white in the darkness. "Looks like it's our lucky day."

They passed through another opening into another cylindrical cavern. Ahead was a tiny waterfall, trickling into a small pool of water.

"Is it safe to drink?" Blaine asked.

"The desert springs are known to be the best sources of water on the planet." Saff crouched and scooped some water to her mouth. Then she reached down and yanked a few twisted plaits of leather off her dress. He watched as she crouched and grabbed two rocks. With expert skill, she struck the rocks together a few times. A spark flared. She kept at it, striking the rocks near the leather ropes until they started to smolder. Soon, they were burning, and she tied them up on the wall.

"This is molexian leather," she said. "It burns well, but slowly. It'll give us some light once the suns set and the rocks stop glowing."

His gaze fell to her long neck and that damn collar. He wanted it gone. He strode up to her and she stilled. He unclicked the collar and tossed the offending item across the cave. It clunked on the rock.

"Thanks," she murmured.

"I've been wanting to do that since I put the damn thing on." He grabbed her arm and lifted it, turning it over so he could see the ugly brand.

Leaning down, he pressed a kiss to it. "This should not be on your skin."

"The same can be said for your scars." She touched one thick ridge on his chest.

Maybe she was right. He'd thought of them as some sort of badge of honor, but as her fingers ran over them, he realized that he was maybe keeping them as a reminder of things that had no place in his new life.

Suddenly, she stepped backward and started stripping off her dress. Blaine froze and watched as she pulled her dress over her head. She was completely unselfconscious.

She made him think of a warrior goddess. She was built to fight, to protect, to defend. He knew she was a champion net fighter, those toned arms capable of deadly precision. He knew she was competitive and never gave up. Her long legs drew his gaze, but so did her flat stomach and her perfectly shaped breasts.

Desire was like a bonfire roaring inside Blaine. For months, he'd had all his choices taken away from him. But right here, right now, Saff was his choice. What he felt for her was his and his alone. What he did with her was his choice and hers.

"Saff." His voice was so choked and deep it was almost unrecognizable.

She was walking toward the water, the muscles flexing in her naked body. Her ass was toned and shapely, and he couldn't take his eyes off it. She stepped into the small pool, wading up to her thighs. She glanced back over her shoulder.

"Come and get me, Earth man." She grinned at him, that smile filled with challenge. "If you can catch me."

He tore his shirt and harness off, dropping them on the ground. "When I catch you, it won't be gentle. It'll be rough. I'll take you hard."

She lifted her chin, standing proud. "Not if I take you first."

Inflamed, he tore open his trousers and shucked them off. Naked, he rushed at her, going after the woman he wanted above all else.

Chapter Eleven

Saff sloshed through the refreshingly cool water, hearing Blaine charge after her. She feinted left before running right, but Blaine kept coming. Like a big predator intent on chasing her down.

The cavern and the pool weren't very big, but she sprinted out of the water, darting across the rocky space. Blaine followed, and when she glanced back, she saw his intense gaze was locked on her.

Stars, that intensity, the primal look in his eyes and the forceful desire pouring off him. No one had ever wanted her the way Blaine did. He put on a burst of speed, and she dodged again, feeling the brush of his fingers on her belly. Using all her agility, she evaded him again. She found so much pleasure in watching his muscles flex. The man should never wear clothes and simply stay naked all the time.

She ignored the bite of rocks under her feet, heading back toward the pool of water. His fingers curled around her hip, and she spun away again. His growl echoed in the confines of the small space.

Saff splashed back into the water, pushing out into the deeper area on the other side of the pool.

But she hadn't gone far when a hand closed around her ankle and jerked her back. Her head slid under the water.

She came up spluttering, and she found her back flush against a hard, male body.

A hard cock prodded against her buttocks. She could feel all of him—that hard chest, muscled thighs, the ripped abs.

"Got you," he growled in her ear.

"Now what?" Her voice was huskier than she'd ever heard it.

His big, callused hands moved up to cup her breasts. As he played with her nipples, Saff bit back a moan. One of his hands slid down her belly.

"I love how strong you are." He touched the tight muscles in her belly, then dragged a hand down her thigh, gripping her. His fingers drifted back up and delved between her thighs. A second later, one thick finger speared inside her. She contracted her inner muscles, felt a flutter of sensation low in her belly.

"I love that I can smell you now, because you smell so good." He brought his fingers to his mouth and licked. "Taste so good."

His fingers were back between her legs and this time he slid a second finger inside her, pumping them in and out of her. He found a rhythm, and that spot inside her that had the pleasure ratcheting up. It burst through her, splotches of light dancing in front of her eyes. He was ruthless, his fingers powering in and out of her.

"Blaine."

"I like when you cry out my name like that. Soft and breathy."

He moved her through the water, toward the edge. He bent her forward, the rock pressing against her hips. His palm smoothed over one of her cheeks and she felt the hard prod of his cock between her folds.

"No," she said.

Behind her, his big body froze.

"I want to see your face," she said quietly. "When you slide inside me."

"Yes." With a growl, he spun her, lifting her bottom up to perch on the edge of the pool. He pushed her legs apart, moving between them, leaning over her.

Saff lay back, uncaring about the small rocks digging into her skin. That pain contrasted with the pleasure pulsing through her.

She looked at Blaine, at his hard, scarred chest, and then she watched as his hand moved down and circled his large erection. He stroked himself, and she licked her lips, desperate for him.

Then her gaze locked with his brown one and he moved forward. The thick head of him nudged between her legs.

"Tell me."

His voice was so guttural she barely understood his words. "What?"

"How I'm going to give it to you."

"Hard," Saff said on a moan. "Rough, and out of control."

With one powerful thrust, he was inside her.

"Yes!" Saff wrapped her legs around his waist, trying to pull him closer.

He thrust once, twice, again and again. Smooth, powerful, overwhelming. Then he pulled out, and pushed her legs farther apart before he sank inside her again.

The intensity of the coupling battered at her. This wasn't sweet or fun. This was hard, tough, and intense. She felt the wild edge riding him, felt the way his big body moved thickly inside her. His pulsing length filled her, bumping that spot deep inside that had her own pleasure spiraling out of control.

"Take me," he said. "All of me."

"Oh, oh... Yes." The words were hissed out of her. A promise.

"I belong here," Blaine said. "Right here. You can handle me, baby, can't you?"

They were both panting, their bodies straining against each other. He was riding her hard, going deep. Saff threw her head back, moaning at the overpowering sensations. She felt like their desires were all tangled up together.

Blaine kept up his punishing pace, his thrusts slamming inside her with a slap of flesh against flesh.

"Oh, drak." Saff felt her orgasm hit her like a net exploding outward. "Yes! Don't stop, Blaine!"

He looked like a man fighting for his sanity. He kept moving and then lodged himself deep, his body stiffening. With a roar, he filled her.

Blaine collapsed beside her, managing to roll

onto his back. Saff fought to get her breathing under control. She felt like she'd fought ten rounds in the arena. She stared up at the rocky ceiling thinking how perfect this moment was: raw, real and free.

***

Blaine stared up at the rocky ceiling of the cavern, filled with regret. Saff deserved better than this.

The last light of the day was gone, but Saff's makeshift torches gave off a faint golden glow.

Beside him, she wriggled a little. She reached out and stroked her hand down his side. His skin was still slick from perspiration.

He moved away and sat up. She did too, pushing all her glorious braids back off her face. She looked almost sweet. Unguarded. This was Saff the beautiful woman, not the gladiator.

She tilted her head. "What's wrong? Let me guess, you were too rough with me?"

Her teasing tone ate at him. "You deserve better than a shitty cave in the middle of nowhere."

She raised a brow. "Do I look like the hearts and flowers type?"

Her breezy tone set off warning bells. "I just want to—"

"Take my choice out of the equation? Give me what you think I want and not what I want?"

He froze. "No. I just wanted things to be nice for you."

"Blaine, you and I are never going to be nice.

And trust me, if anyone calls me nice, I'll hit them. I like what we have. I enjoy you, I enjoy us. Hard, fast and a little rough."

Before he could respond, she climbed into his lap, facing him. Her hands reached down, cupping his already hardening cock. She stroked him a few times and Blaine bit back a moan.

Then she lifted her hips until the hard head of him was lodged in her folds.

"I'm hungry," she said.

In that moment, getting inside her was more important than anything ever before. With her strong body poised over him, their gazes locked. Then she slid down on him.

A groan ripped out of Blaine's chest and he thrust his hips up. His hands clenched on her tight ass, while hers dug into his shoulders, her nails biting into his skin.

Saff moved up and down, faster and faster. She spread her thighs wide across him, working his cock in and out of her tight body.

He had the most perfect fucking view. Her eyes were bright, glazed with desire. The muscles in her body flexed with each rise of her hips. She moved faster and faster, and Blaine's chest tightened.

Then she arched her back, her breasts thrust forward, and her body clamped down on him. She screamed his name.

Blaine had never seen anything more beautiful.

A second later he reached up, his fingers biting into her ass as he slammed her down one last time. He came with a fierce shout that echoed off the walls around them.

They collapsed against each other and somehow, Blaine found the strength to move them back toward their discarded clothes. He dozed and when he drifted awake again, Saff was snuggled into his side, snoring softly.

He grinned. Saff Essikani snored. God, she was perfect.

He carefully pulled away from her and grabbed his trousers. He wondered if he'd have any luck finding them something to eat.

A while later, he was carefully cooking some meat over one of Saff's torches. He'd found some mushroom-like growths in the tunnel and spent a hell of a long time chasing a small lizard around. Damn thing better taste good.

"Don't eat the plants."

Saff's sleep-husky voice made him look over his shoulder. Immediately, his cock jumped.

She was sprawled out, completely naked, her head propped up on one hand. There wasn't a lick of self-consciousness about her.

"There isn't much to choose from," he said.

"They're poisonous. They'll dissolve your insides."

Right. He grabbed the mushrooms and tossed them away. "The lizard?"

"Should be delicious."

He brought the seared meat over to her. "You going to put some clothes on?"

She raised a brow. "Why? I'm planning to fuck you again once I'm finished eating."

Blaine wolfed down his pieces of meat in record time. In his head, he had visions of taking Saff from behind or her riding him—hard and fast—into sweet oblivion.

"So, I guess this is what Rory calls a date?" Saff said.

Blaine made a scoffing sound. "Women on Earth expect a little more than a rocky cave and grilled lizard."

Saff smiled. "I like it."

"I suppose your pretty boys take you fancy places." God, Blaine wanted to strangle every man who'd touched her.

"No. I've never had a man make a meal for me or take me somewhere fancy."

He looked at her across the smoldering flames of the torch. "Then the men of Carthago are Grade-A idiots."

"You're good for my ego, Blaine Strong." Saff's smile dissolved. "I'm glad you're with me."

He reached for her, pulling her long body into his. He expected the usual explosion of heat and desire, but as he touched her, another need overtook him. He stroked her, slow and easy, caressing each dip and curve of her. She moaned, moving under his hands. He sucked her nipples into his mouth, taking his time to find the perfect pressure and what drove her to cry out his name. He slid his hands between her legs, stroking where she was wet and needy.

The desire that slammed into him was as brutal as before, but this time, he controlled it, keeping his touch gentle.

She kept nipping at him, shimmying her body against him, and he knew she expected hard and fast.

But they'd done hard, fast and rough, and this time he wanted something else.

"Blaine." An impatient, frustrated moan.

He caressed her face, settling himself between her thighs. She turned her head and sucked his thumb into her mouth. *Damn*. He almost lost it.

"Hang on, baby, I'm going to take care of you." He'd fill her up and take her over, and give her something he suspected she'd never had before.

He hitched her long legs around his waist and then was thrusting deep inside her. She made a mewling sound and arched into him. As he thrust his cock inside her, her hips jerked up to meet him. God, she was so tight, clutching him hard. He kept up his deep, slow thrusts.

"Blaine...I..." She arched her back, her gaze locking with his. "I feel—"

As her climax washed over her, he felt her heels digging into his back. Watching the emotions spill across her face pushed him over the edge.

His orgasm was almost painful as it tore through him. And three things echoed in his head.

Mine. More. Saff.

***

Saff woke, feeling bruised and battered and wonderful. She rolled over, curling into Blaine's hard body, and inhaled the scent of his skin. After their first few frenzied couplings, and after he'd almost destroyed her with his slow, sexy lovemaking, she'd been sure neither of them would be up for more. But they'd turned to each other through the night, again and again.

Stars, the man knew just how to bring her to her knees.

She'd felt his strong desire time and again, but during the night, when he'd rocked slowly inside her, she'd felt some other emotion as well. It had been something she'd never felt before: strong, warm, and good. It had wrapped around her and she wasn't sure if it had been her feeling, his, or both.

Suddenly, she heard noises outside the cave, and realized that was what had woken her. Frowning, she noted the faint light filtering in from above. It had to be sunrise.

"Blaine." She nudged him.

He woke quickly, frowning as he also heard the voices echoing in the canyon.

Quickly, they pulled on their clothes and crept back through the tunnel to the cave entrance. Down below, a convoy was moving through the winding path of the canyon. Large, lumbering animals covered in shaggy, matted, white fur were pulling a long row of carts that bumped over the ground.

All the carts carried cages filled with women.

Saff's hands clenched on the rock wall. *Drak.* There were so many of them.

Blaine held up a hand, pointing down toward some larger boulders at the bottom of the canyon that they could use for cover. She nodded. After the convoy had passed the mouth of their cave, they carefully snuck down the slope, making sure to avoid any attention.

She raced in behind one of the large rocks, pressing her back against it. Then Blaine pointed again. Together, they darted from one rock to another, getting closer to the convoy.

At this range, Saff had a better view of the cages. They looked like they were made of bone and metal. Her stomach churned. The prisoners were made up of females of various alien species, in varying conditions. Some looked well-fed and strong, others emaciated and starved. One or two were cradling swollen, pregnant bellies. Saff tried to shelve the unruly emotions battering her. Her gaze fell on one small form in a cage near the back of the convoy.

She sucked in a breath and nudged Blaine.

It was Winter.

Saff's gaze darted to the front of the convoy, rapidly searching the cages again. Her shoulders fell. There was no sign of Dayna or Mia.

Suddenly, rough male voices sounded, and Saff spotted guards walking toward the back of the convoy.

"They're going to be happy with this new batch."

The pair of guards laughed.

"There are a few I'd spend my coin on." The taller of the guards pushed a hand through the bars of one cage to touch a woman.

"Rotting scum." The woman spat through the cage bars.

The shorter, stockier guard swung a staff around and banged it against the bars. "We'll see how you like it at Zaabha."

Saff's eyes widened. It couldn't be. It was only a myth.

"Got a ways to go yet," the taller guard said. "Today we have to reach the Rishyk Trading Post before night hits, but tomorrow..." He laughed, the sound coarse and meaningful.

"We've got to get them out," Blaine whispered.

Saff stared at the convoy, analyzing its composition. There were only six guards in total, but they were all armed. Still, there would be more guards at the trading post, so they had better odds of freeing Winter and the other slaves here.

Nodding, Saff pointed to the pair of guards closest to them. "We take these two down first, and get their weapons. Then we attack the other four."

Blaine nodded. They looked at each other and counted down.

Together, they spun out from behind the boulder, and raced toward the closest guards. Blaine slammed a fist into the stocky guard's lower back. Saff jumped into the air, as high as she could. The taller guard was turning to face her, when she wrapped her strong legs around his neck.

With a twist of her thighs, she broke his neck. He didn't even get a chance to shout or draw his weapon. She rode his body to the ground.

When she looked up, Blaine was there, holding out a hand to her. His guard was lying facefirst amongst the rocks.

"You are amazing," Blaine murmured.

She leaned down and yanked a sword from the guard's scabbard. It was inferior to her own weapons, but it would have to do. She glanced at Blaine. "You can tell me that later, Earth man." She grabbed a sword off the second guard's body and handed it to him.

Shouts sounded from the start of the convoy. She looked up and saw three guards charging toward them.

"Ready?" she asked.

Blaine spun his blade. "Oh, yeah."

Saff met the first guard, her sword clanging against his. After three thrusts, she knew he wasn't very skilled with the weapon. With a thrust through the gut, she took her guard down. She glanced toward Blaine, to see that he had engaged the next two guards.

As she turned to locate the remaining guard, she heard a twang, followed by a whistle of sound. It was all-too-familiar, after their interaction with the Corsair Caravan. She glanced up to see an arrow arching through the sky in their direction.

Damn, the final guard had kept his distance, and he had a bow.

The arrow missed them, landing nearby, but a second later it exploded. Rocks flew in every direction. Saff fell to the ground, throwing her arms over her head. She heard someone cry out.

When the rain of rocks and debris stopped, she raised her head. Blaine was crouched nearby. One of his guards was down and bleeding, the other one had been hit in the head by a large rock.

Another arrow flew through the air, landing with a similar wild explosion. Saff crouched down near the cages. The bastard was using explosive-tipped arrows. The caged women were all crying out in terror.

She had to stop the bowman.

Saff climbed up on top of the closest cage. The guard was firing close to the convoy, but she didn't think he'd fire on the slaves. Ignoring the frightened faces below, she ran across the cages, keeping her balance.

An arrow flew past her, close enough for her to feel the rush of air, but she kept running. Then she leaped off the cages and slammed into the bowman, before he could fire another arrow.

As they crashed into the ground, the man cursed. A quick scuffle, an elbow to his chin, and he dropped back, dazed. She lifted her sword and slammed the hilt against his head, until his eyes rolled back and he slumped down.

She turned around to see that Blaine was already opening the cages. She joined him and they grinned at each other.

"Three guards apiece," he said.

She made a scoffing sound. "Three for me, two for you. One of yours got hit by a flying rock."

He cupped the back of her skull and yanked her in for a quick, hard kiss. "I am crazy about you."

From the cages, women were calling out. Saff touched a smear of blood on his cheek. "I can't wait to get back to the House of Galen. I have plans."

He smiled. "Me too."

They turned back to the women and soon hurried to Winter's cage. Blaine reached through the bars. "Are you okay, Winter?"

"Blaine?" The woman let out a small cry, turning her sightless eyes toward them. "I heard the commotion but—" her chest hitched "—I had no idea what was going on."

"We're going to get you out of here," he said. "Saff and I are here. We'll—"

Suddenly, there were the sounds of galloping hooves. Saff turned her head, her muscles tensing.

"There were more guards riding ahead of the convoy," Winter said urgently.

Drak. Saff used a few other curses in her head. They should have known. She saw a group of guards riding *tarnids* appear. An entire armed platoon.

No. Saff scanned the steep walls of the canyon. There was nowhere to go. Some of the freed women starting running, some trying to scale the slopes.

Saff looked at Blaine. They both knew they couldn't take all these guards. They were outnumbered and outmatched.

The guards thundered in, some snatching up the fleeing women and tossing them across their beasts. They circled around where Blaine and Saff stood. One *tarnid* moved forward and Saff's jaw went tight.

"My champion returns."

She glared at the Srinar from the fortress in Gaia. He was wearing another purple shirt and smiling at Blaine. They should have killed him when they'd had the chance.

She saw her own angry frustration reflected in Blaine's eyes.

Together, they dropped their swords and raised their hands.

Chapter Twelve

The hard blow slammed into Blaine's midsection. He jerked against the two Srinar guards holding him upright. Then he turned his head and spat blood out onto the rocky ground.

"Are your reinforcements close?" The Srinar leader asked.

"Fuck you," Blaine answered.

He got another punch to his gut. The fucking guard had some sort of metal on his knuckles and Blaine was pretty sure he had a few cracked ribs. Pain radiated through him, but he stomped it down, like he had a million times before in the fight rings.

Nearby, Saff jerked against her captors, but then stilled.

"Where is Galen?" the leader asked again.

This time Blaine remained silent.

More punches pummeled into him, and blood pooled in his mouth. He glared at the guards, daring them to do their worst.

"Enough." The leader stared at Blaine with black eyes. "He's too drakking tough." The man spun and strode over to Saff. He stroked a hand down her arm and she raised a brow at him.

Looking like a queen staring down at a peasant.

The leader pulled a knife from the scabbard on the belt of one of the nearby guards. He held the blade against the skin of her bicep.

"I applaud your choice of woman," the leader said to Blaine. "I like a warrior in my bed."

Fucking asshole. Rage boiled inside Blaine. If the bastard hurt Saff...

"Actually, I picked him," Saff said. "I like a real man in my bed." Her tone left no doubt that she found the Srinar man lacking.

Blaine was shocked at the laugh that threatened. God, she was something.

"I'll ask you again." The Srinar tugged at his purple shirt, straightening it. "What's your plan? How many reinforcements do you have coming?"

Blaine just stared at the man.

The leader shook his head and lifted the knife again. He moved it down Saff's arm. She hissed but didn't move. A cut opened up, blood dripping down her glossy skin.

The side of Blaine he'd struggled to control and accept since his captivity roared to life. He heaved in air, fighting for some control. He couldn't lose it here. He had to stay in control for Saff.

"Hmm, you are a tough one," the leader said to Saff. "But I'm very good at knowing what can break a man or woman."

The leader nodded at some other guards, and suddenly Winter's small body was dropped on the ground in front of them. She fell onto her knees, her face pale and dirty. She moved her head, her milky eyes looking off past them as she strained to hear what was happening.

"Blaine? Saff?"

"We're here," Blaine told her.

"Don't tell them anything," Winter said bravely.

The leader lifted his sword, standing behind Winter. Blaine's gut went hard as a rock, his chest constricting.

"Wait." No fucking way he'd let this woman die here in the dirt on this alien world.

"No, Blaine." Saff struggled again. "Don't tell them anything."

But Blaine looked at Winter. They were going to hurt her, and the woman didn't deserve any more pain or suffering.

"There are no reinforcements. We escaped from the Gaia Oasis, just the two of us, and we're alone out here."

The Srinar leader smiled. "Good. Good. Lock them all up." He spun, reaching out to stroke Saff's face. "You'll make a lovely fight slave in the Zaabha Arena."

"That's where you moved your fight rings," she spat.

"Yes. I lose some of the District visitors, but the most enthusiastic will make the journey into the desert. And there will be no more pesky imperators bothering me."

"That's what you think," Saff bit out.

Blaine growled, watching as Saff kicked out a foot at the leader. He stumbled back, scowling at her. Then the guards dragged her toward a cage.

She fought the entire way, her struggles getting wilder and more savage. He saw her face, and it shattered his heart. She hated the idea of being locked up again. Caged like an animal.

Blaine was tossed into a cage, and Winter was forced in after him. After a wild fight, Saff was pushed into the cage beside them. She grabbed the bars, rattling them, trying to stop them from closing the door.

"Saff." Blaine moved as close as he could. "Saff, it's okay."

She didn't react to his voice, and when the guards slammed her cage door closed, she let out a wild yell that echoed in the canyon.

***

The hot suns beat down on them as the convoy rattled up the rocky path. Saff sat with her knees pressed to her chest, forcing back the ugly panic clawing at her insides.

Her father had liked to cage her when she wasn't fighting. Keep her mean and hungry.

She'd tested the bars. They were made of metal and a tough bone that was extremely strong.

She heard the quiet murmur of a deep voice. Blaine's voice. She stared through the bars, watching him trying to comfort Winter. The small human woman had wilted, her face incredibly pale.

His head lifted and their gazes met.

"You okay?" he asked.

"No." She kicked at the bars. She hated them.

But as she looked at Blaine's tense shoulders and stark face, she could see that being a captive again was hurting him, too. She reached a hand through the bars.

He grabbed it tight, his fingers tangling with hers.

"Not alone, Earth man." She knew Galen would be tearing Gaia apart, searching for them. She breathed deep. She hoped the imperator could find them.

Finally, the convoy rolled to a halt. Gut tight, she thought they'd reached their destination. But as the guard moved down the row of cages, handing small cups of water to the captives, she realized it was just a short break.

She took the small, beaten cup and gulped the water back. It barely lubricated her dry throat. She watched Blaine help Winter take a cup, and then he reached for one.

Suddenly, two guards gripped Blaine's arms and yanked him hard against the bars of the cage. Saff moved into a crouch, fighting to control herself. Blaine tried to jerk back, but they held him tight.

"You've missed this, haven't you?" The Srinar leader was back, and he was holding up a pressure injector.

No! Saff bit down on her lip to stop from crying out. She hated feeling helpless.

Blaine roared and struggled. The leader leaned forward and jammed the injector against Blaine's neck.

"And I'll just leave this one here for you, too."

The man left a second injector on the floor beside Blaine. "For when you succumb to the need for more." He turned away, laughing with his men.

Blaine gripped the bars, the muscles in his arms and chest straining. Saff saw he was gritting his teeth, his veins standing out against his skin. She felt an ugly blackness throbbing off him.

Winter scuttled backward, clearly sensing something was wrong.

Saff reached out, her hand brushing Blaine's skin. It felt burning hot.

"Blaine?"

He tried to pull away, but she wrapped her fingers around his arm and held on. She wouldn't abandon him.

"You're okay." She kept her voice calm. "Winter, stay back."

The woman nodded, keeping to the far side of the small cage. She was afraid, but there was a determined look on her face. "I could help…"

"It's okay, he's beaten this addiction. He'll get through this."

His big body trembled, a choked sound escaping his chest.

"He needs to remember who he is," Winter said. Her calm, sensible words made Saff remember the woman had been a healer back on Earth. "All the reasons he has not to give in to his addiction."

Saff nodded. "Look at me." She said the words with the snap of authority in her voice. "Look at me, Earth man."

His eyes lifted. The deep brown looked paler, wilder.

"You are Blaine Strong. You're a man from Earth, a fighter, a survivor, a champion, and a gladiator of the House of Galen."

He pulled in a deep breath, his chest shuddering.

"You're my lover, and the man I choose to fight beside." Emotion made her voice husky. He was hers. Not just for the bed sport, but so much more. Somehow, this tough, stubborn human had burrowed in under her guard and she'd never even noticed. No, that was wrong. She'd noticed and she'd wanted it to happen. Saff realized that for the first time in her life, she was falling in love.

Proper love. Not the twisted travesty her mother had believed was love.

"Hurts," he choked out.

She reached up, stroking a hand through his hair. "I know." She ran her fingers along his jaw. "You're stronger with the drugs in your system." Drak, she hated to ask this of him, but she *knew* he could embrace this new part of himself and use it. "You need to embrace it, Blaine. Use the strength and bend the bars. If you can bend them enough, we can get out."

He nodded, but the movement was slow as he fought through the fog of the drugs.

Then he turned, his broad back blocking the bars from the view of the guards not too far away. He gripped the bars and started to pull them apart. He strained, air whistling between his teeth.

Come on. Saff watched and willed her own strength into him. The bars started to bend and sweat poured down his body.

"I'm out of control." He looked back over his shoulder, his eyes churning with emotions. "I could hurt someone. I could hurt you."

"Embrace it, Blaine. Use it."

His chin dropped to his chest. He pulled against the bars and she saw them move a fraction more.

He kept going, and soon there was enough room for him and Winter to squeeze through.

"You did it," Saff whispered.

Blaine reached over and grabbed Winter's arm. "Time to go, Winter."

The woman nodded, pushing her tangled hair back. She put all her trust in Blaine and let him help her through the bars. Saff felt a stab of admiration. The woman couldn't see a thing, but she was trusting them with her life.

Blaine climbed out and turned to Saff's cage.

That's when she saw him stagger. *Drak.* The effects of the drug were wearing off.

He grabbed the bars in front of her, and started pulling on them. She saw his muscles straining. The bars only moved the tiniest amount. Saff's throat went dry. She wanted out.

But when he sagged against her cage, Winter moved in and jammed her shoulder into his side to keep him upright. Now, Saff tasted panic.

Determination made Blaine's face stark. He grabbed the bars and heaved again and again. They didn't move. She placed her hands next to his and tried to help. Together they strained, but the metal bars were too strong.

Saff squeezed her eyes closed, but then she felt the crash of Blaine's chaotic emotions. When she opened them, Blaine had a terrible look on his face.

He was staring at the second injector lying on the floor of his abandoned cage.

"If I take another dose, I'll have no control," he said. "A second one always makes it worse. I won't even remember my name."

There was so much torment in him, and so many nightmares, in his eyes. His greatest horrors lay in the drugs that had stolen the man he'd once been.

Saff let out a shaky breath. "Don't take it." She wrapped her hands around his. "I can sense what you feel, Blaine. Don't take it."

A vicious shake of his head. "I won't leave you."

"And I won't risk what a second dose might do to you."

His face spasmed, then he reached toward the cage and the second injection.

Suddenly, shouts rang from the nearby guards. They'd been spotted.

"There's no time." Saff forced herself to find her calm. Even if he took it now, there was no time to bend the bars. "Go! Get Winter to safety."

"No."

Saff smacked the bars. "You have to protect her. Now, go!"

Blaine's tormented eyes met hers through the bars. "Saff—"

Arrows hit the cages near them, and some of the

other prisoners screamed.

"Go!" Saff roared at him.

Blaine wrapped an arm around Winter. "I'm coming back for you, Saff."

Then he turned and half carried the blind woman into the rocks.

***

He was sweltering, his mouth dry as dust, but Blaine kept putting one foot in front of the other.

He was out in the middle of a giant plain of sand dunes. His boots kept slipping on the sand, and with each step, he wondered if he'd finally lose his footing and not get back up.

Winter had collapsed hours ago and he was carrying her in his arms.

But his thoughts were with Saff.

He'd left her. She was somewhere far behind him, still locked away. Still a prisoner.

He'd managed to evade the guards, and hide himself and Winter among the rocks. Eventually, the guards had stopped searching for them, and he'd headed in the opposite direction to the convoy. Every step away from Saff had been like walking on razorblades.

All his fault. He knew what would happen to her. She'd be taken to Zaabha and be forced to fight. Forced to relive her worst nightmares.

He'd left her there.

His hesitation in taking the drugs had lost him the chance to rescue her, his woman. The one woman who challenged and supported him, who'd never seen him as a monster.

Blaine wanted to roar out his pain and frustration, but his mouth was too dry, and the last of his energy was dwindling.

He hadn't gone much farther when he dropped to his knees. He clutched Winter tightly, so she didn't tumble to the sand. God, he'd failed to protect her, *and* he'd failed Saff.

"I'm so sorry, Saff," he murmured.

As he knelt there, he waited for death to take him. The sunlight stabbed into his eyes and when he saw shimmering shapes ahead, he knew it was a hallucination brought on by the heat.

He closed his eyes. In his head, he was back in the cave with Saff. Both of them submerged in the cool water as he slid inside her tight body.

"*Drak*," a male voice said.

Blaine frowned. That wasn't right. That wasn't part of his fantasy.

He heard the snorts of beasts and the murmur of voices. He forced his heavy eyelids open, and saw the face of Galen, with his black patch over one eye.

Behind the imperator was a cluster of *tarnids,* as well as an armored desert vehicle hovering just above the ground.

Suddenly, Raiden was there, kneeling in front of Blaine, the tattooed gladiator holding up a water bladder to Blaine's lips. As the water slid down his throat, he gulped it as fast as he could.

Nero appeared, taking Winter from Blaine's arms. "I'll take care of her."

Blaine managed a nod. "Saff." He looked up at Galen's icy-blue gaze. "They have Saff."

Galen's face hardened. "A mistake I'm sure she'll make them regret."

"They have her locked up." Blaine pushed the water away, his stomach protesting. "They are taking her to Zaabha." He heard sharp intakes of breath all around him.

"Zaabha doesn't exist," Galen said.

"It's real." Blaine struggled to get up. Kace and Harper appeared, and gripped his arms. He stood, hating that he felt so weak. "They were stopping at a trading post for the night, then going on to Zaabha."

The imperator cursed. "Rishyk is the closest trading post."

Harper patted Blaine's arm. "Glad you're okay."

He wasn't. He wouldn't be, until Saff was free. He turned his head and caught Kace's gaze. He saw the concern in Saff's fight partner's eyes.

"We have to get to her," Blaine said.

"I will," Kace answered. "You're in no shape—"

"She's mine." The sharp words fell between them. "I left her there, and I have to get her back."

Galen pressed a hand to the back of his neck and muttered a curse. "Stubborn asses who fall in love." He shook his head. "You need a stimulant to keep you on your feet, Blaine. You okay with that?"

This time Blaine didn't hesitate. It wasn't the same as the drugs the Srinar had used. It wasn't the drugs he'd been addicted to and fought to be free of. And right now, he'd do anything to rescue Saff.

"Do it." He gritted his teeth, as Lore brought the shot and jabbed it into Blaine's bicep. He instantly felt the energy wash through him, chasing out his exhaustion. "How's Winter?"

Not far away, he saw Winter sitting with Nero in the vehicle, conscious, and taking small sips of water that the big gladiator held to her lips. She looked so small, held in Nero's bulging arms.

Nero nodded. "She's weak, but she'll recover."

"Someone needs to take Winter back to Kor Magna," Galen said.

"No." The woman's voice was quiet but firm. "You'll lose a fighter, and you'll need them all to rescue Saff."

"You're too weak," Nero grumbled. "You're a liability."

The small woman turned a glare up at him, the effect not diluted by her milky-white eyes. "I'll stay out of your way. You'll need everyone to get in and find Saff, and Dayna, and Mia."

"They were with you?" Galen asked.

Winter nodded. "We were separated into different convoys heading to Zaabha. They're out here, somewhere."

Galen nodded. "Okay. Winter will ride with Nero. Blaine, you take that *tarnid*." He pointed to one of the large beasts. "Let's move out."

Chapter Thirteen

Dark was falling when the convoy reached the Rishyk Trading Post.

In the growing gloom, Saff couldn't see very much of the place, but she took note of vertical rock walls rising up—colored in bands of cream, red, and black. She also saw plenty of fences made from bones, and cages stacked high. All around the enclosure, torches had been lit, and the hides of skinned animals hung to dry, desert insects buzzing around them.

The snorts, howls, and yips of different animals echoed into the night. As she stared at the huge bones that had been used as fence posts, she couldn't even imagine what beast they'd come from. She knew she really didn't want to meet a live one.

As their convoy jerked to a halt, she saw rows of cages stacked three high. They were filled with women.

Soon, guards started offloading the cages, and stacking them with the others. As her cage was moved, she looked upward. Through the bars, she saw the stars overhead.

All of a sudden, her cage lurched, and one end hit the ground. She tumbled, slamming against the bars. One of the bars was damaged and she felt the stab of metal in her side.

"Watch it, Mrat," the other guard snapped.

"It slipped. This one is heavy."

Her cage was righted, and she was slid into place with the other cages.

"When we reach Zaabha, they'll make us fight, and we'll die."

The defeated voice made Saff look through to the cage neighboring hers. A tough-looking alien woman sat there, her green hair falling to her waist. It was matted and ratty. Her skin was a paler green covering a flat chest, and had a faint scale pattern. Despair wafted off her.

Saff took a few deep breaths. She'd been here before, locked up and forced to fight. She'd survived and she would again. "So we'll fight."

The other woman shook her head. "The Zaabha crowds are bloodthirsty. Vicious." The woman's voice wavered. "And there is a brutal champion. A woman with no mercy."

Saff took another deep breath of the warm desert air. "I'll bow before no champion." She was Saff Essikani, best net fighter in the Kor Magna Arena. She wouldn't forget that.

But as she settled in, listening to the sounds of the trading post—raucous laughter in the distance, the sobs of women in the cages, and the snorts of restless beasts—she felt so alone. She missed her team, her friends, Blaine.

She was once again alone...but this time, she was no longer a frightened child.

She shifted, and felt a flare of pain in her side. Touching her hip, she found a tear in the leather of her dress, and a sticky spot that had to be blood. *Drak*. She probed the wound. Not bad. It could wait.

Her thoughts turned to Blaine and Winter. She hoped they'd gotten away and were safe. Saff dragged her knees up to her chest. She knew the desert could be unforgiving. Blaine had made the right decision to leave and protect Winter. He'd done what Saff had demanded...but *drak*, she hated being left alone in this cage.

She rubbed her cheek on her knee. Enough of the self-pity. If Blaine had made it back to Galen and the others, they would come for her.

She wasn't really alone. She closed her eyes and thought of Blaine's touch. All the things they'd done to each other by that little pool in the cave. It was so easy to remember the feel of him moving inside her, especially when she still felt the faint twinges of their energetic loving.

Blaine would come for her. She knew it in her heart.

But as she studied the long line of cages, she realized that he might be too late. If they left in the morning and arrived at Zaabha, he might not find her.

She straightened her legs. Enough. It was drakking time to rescue herself.

She moved over to the bar that had been damaged in the fall, carefully exploring it with her fingertips. The bone part was still intact, but the metal part had splintered. She poked at it, gently prying off a thin sliver of metal. She held it up in the dim torchlight, studying it. This might work. Moving to the door, she stuck the sliver in the lock, and set to work trying to pick it.

"What are you doing?" The alien woman murmured frantically from beside her.

"I'm leaving."

"There's nowhere to go. The desert night beasts will eat you alive. And in the daytime, the suns will bake you."

"I'll take my chances."

With a quiet click, her cell door swung open.

Elation rocketed through her. Carefully, Saff climbed out, stretching her aching muscles. Then she moved over and quickly picked the woman's lock.

"It's your choice," Saff said.

She looked at the other cages, and wished she could risk freeing everybody. But if she did, it was much less likely that any of them would manage to get away. They'd likely all end up back in the cages. She swore to herself that she would find a way to come back and free all of these poor women.

In a crouch, she hurried over to one of the fences. Inside the partition, several animals were pacing around. Some sort of hunting cats, by the look of them. She snapped a large piece of bone off the fence. She hefted it, testing its weight. It wasn't much of a weapon, but it would have to do.

Spinning, she snuck away into the darkness.

***

Nero

Nero held Winter in his arms as they traveled on the *tarnid*. Night was falling, and he was eager to get to the trading post. He knew that the open desert was the favorite hunting ground of the night beasts.

He looked down at the sleeping woman in his arms. She'd fallen asleep a while back, slumping back against him. He tightened his arms around her and sniffed. She was so slight, so delicate.

Women on his world of Symeria were almost as big as the males. Strength was prized, and sickly, small babies didn't survive the planet's harsh climes.

Winter shivered, and he reached in his saddlebags and pulled out his fur cloak. He wrapped it around her, and saw her slender fingers reach out to stroke the soft, gray fur.

"Thank you," she said quietly. She tipped her head up, and his gaze dropped to her sweet smile and that terrible white film over her useless eyes. "It smells like you."

He grunted, guessing that her lack of vision had enhanced her other senses. "You should have returned to Kor Magna."

Her smile disappeared. "Did you want to miss the mission?"

No, he didn't. Nero wanted blood, and he wanted Saff back. They had to right the wrong of the attack on the House of Galen, and the abduction of the human women who'd been stolen from them.

On his world, a barbarian warlord was required to show his strength and protect his people.

"You can stash me somewhere when we reach the trading post," Winter said.

He frowned, disliking the idea of her huddled alone in the darkness with no protection. "You shouldn't be here."

She stiffened. "Because I'm blind? Useless?"

On Symeria, she would be considered inadequate, weak, a hindrance. "Yes. You're small, lacking in strength, and without sight, you can't add value."

She sucked in a shocked breath. "And you're an asshole."

There was a bite to her voice that made him raise a brow. "On my world, the small and weak don't survive. They are a burden."

She shot him a fierce look. "A barbarian world, right?" She snorted. "I'm not surprised you're so unenlightened."

Nero frowned. The bite in her voice had turned razor sharp.

"You prize physical strength above all else. No matter what someone has to offer."

"My world has always needed strength. It has a harsh environment."

Winter turned to look ahead, even though he knew her damaged eyes couldn't see the vista before them. "Do you know what I did before the Thraxians stole me, experimented on me, and blinded me? Before they made me a *burden*?"

Nero felt the lick of an uncomfortable emotion. "No."

"I was a doctor."

A healer. He hadn't known that. He'd looked at her and just seen her delicate bone structure and lack of sight.

But he'd always been honest with himself. He'd also noticed her stubborn chin, pale skin, and inky-black hair.

"Save your arrogant views, barbarian. I don't have time for idiots who are all brawn and no brains."

Nero stiffened, but stayed silent. *Maddening Earth woman.* Regardless of her thoughts, she was a member of the House of Galen now. He'd protect her, whether she wanted it or not. And whether she liked him or not was irrelevant.

***

Blaine and the others moved into the mouth of the rocky canyon. Sharp cliffs rose on either side of them, and ahead, he saw a faint glow. The trading post.

I'm coming, Saff. They were almost there. Their plan was to sneak into the trading post, locate Saff, and search for any hint of Dayna and Mia. Preferably, they'd avoid a confrontation.

Blaine scowled into the darkness. It was a shame. He wanted to spill some blood.

Suddenly, Nero jerked his *tarnid* to a halt. The

big man scanned the darkness around them. "Something's hunting us."

Blaine drew his sword, turning in the saddle. He saw Winter, stiff and wide-eyed, in the circle of Nero's arms, a fur cloak around her shoulders.

The other gladiators closed in, drawing their weapons.

"What is it?" Galen asked.

Nero shook his head. "Not sure. Something big."

Blaine couldn't hear or sense anything. "You're sure?"

"Nero's the best tracker I've seen, and also an experienced hunter," Lore said. "If he says something's out there, he's right."

Blaine searched the darkness again, but still didn't see anything. He caught Harper's gaze, and the woman gave a slight shake of her head.

Then Blaine caught a glimpse of movement in the darkness, off to the side. Something big. He straightened in his saddle. "There—"

The gladiators all swiveled, and Harper lifted the burning torch she held.

Suddenly, a masculine shout broke the tension, followed by a high-pitched, feminine scream.

They all spun.

Blaine saw the giant black creature leap out of the darkness and slam into Nero and Winter. The animal knocked the pair off their *tarnid*. Nero curled his body around Winter as they fell.

Fuck. Blaine slid off his *tarnid* and ran toward them, Harper and Raiden flanking him.

Somewhere in the darkness, he heard Galen shouting.

On the ground, Winter was screaming. Blaine knew that the blind woman must be frantic, unable to see what was attacking her.

Blaine spotted the large, lizard-like creature. It had sharp fangs locked into the fur that was wrapped around Winter, dragging her away. There was no sign of Nero.

Together, the House of Galen gladiators ran forward. The lizard looked up, hissing at them. Then Nero charged out of the shadows, hefting an axe. He hacked at the creature.

The others surrounded it, backing up Nero. Blaine jabbed at the beast with his sword, while the others stabbed and sliced.

Nero ducked in, grabbed Winter, and wrenched the woman free. She was trembling, clutching at Nero's shoulders.

He scooped her close to his chest. "I have you."

Galen stepped closer to the lizard, striking it through the neck. It was a killing blow. The lizard dropped to the ground, green blood flowing onto the sand. Its scales shone darkly under the torchlight.

"Ugly thing." Thorin hefted his axe over his shoulder, and gave the creature a kick.

Galen moved toward his agitated *tarnid*, tugging on the reins to calm the beast. "Let's keep moving, before anything else tries to eat us for dinner."

They moved onward and not long after, the glow of the trading post grew in intensity. They left their *tarnids* hidden amongst some rocks with Winter.

"You're sure you'll be okay?" Harper asked.

Winter nodded. "I survived a giant-lizard attack. I'll be fine." She lifted a slim shoulder. "Besides, I don't mind the dark. I'm always in the dark."

Blaine hated leaving her, but was eager to get to Saff. Surprisingly, he saw Nero was reluctant to leave Winter, too, but the way the woman blatantly ignored the big gladiator made him wonder what had transpired between the two of them.

Their group rounded a turn in the canyon and crouched down. Blaine squinted against the glow of the burning torches ahead, and stared at the rough, stone buildings of the trading post. A bone fence circled the settlement.

He also saw the stacked cages, and his jaw tightened.

"Looks like everyone is sleeping," Galen murmured. "Split up. Search for Saff, and any sign of Dayna and Mia. Let's try not to gain anyone's attention, unless we have to."

Blaine felt a focused sensation flow over him. He ran ahead, darting through the shadows, making his way toward the cages.

Suddenly, a Srinar guard rounded a corner. The man's single eye widened, his mouth opening to alert the others.

Blaine leaped on him, dragging him to the ground and out of view of anybody else. He pressed his knee hard against the man's throat, listening to his harsh sounds as he fought for air.

"My woman—dark skin with braided hair. She's a fighter. Where is she?"

The guard gurgled.

Blaine eased off a little, lifting his sword and pressing the tip to the man's neck until blood ran down his skin.

"Shout for help and you die." He pressed harder. "Where is she?"

"Cages at the back. Near the end."

Blaine nodded, lifted his sword, and slammed the hilt into the man's temple. Blaine got to his feet and raced down the line of cages. So many women. Some were asleep, while others sobbed quietly in the darkness. The blood in his veins turned to ice. He knew he couldn't leave them here.

Finally, he reached the end of the cages. He passed one that held a green-haired woman, and stopped at the next one.

His chest constricted to a tight ball.

It was empty.

Chapter Fourteen

Saff crept through the darkness, making a silent vow to come back to the trading post and free the other women.

But first, she needed to escape.

She touched the wound on her side, and realized she was bleeding more heavily than she thought. *Drak.* She was starting to feel light-headed.

She wouldn't survive long once the suns came up if she was already feeling weak. She leaned against a rock wall to rest for a second. She needed an animal to ride out of here. She wouldn't get far on foot.

Glancing across the trading post, she stared at the larger bone fences. That had to be where the beasts of burden were kept by the guards and traders. Now she just had to cross the settlement without getting caught.

She moved along the rock wall, circling closer. A scrape of noise behind her caught her ear, and she tensed. Someone was following her.

Tightening her grip on her bone weapon, she picked up speed. But another noise, closer this time made her realize she wasn't going to outrun whoever was after her.

She turned, holding the bone up. She sensed a hint of emotion: grim determination.

A big, hulking shape came out of the darkness. She swung the bone.

It connected. She heard a masculine grunt. She swung out with a front kick, her foot hitting a rock-hard stomach.

But her opponent moved. Fast. He spun under her guard, and strong arms banded around her.

She thrust her head back, cracking against the man's face.

A strangled groan. "Saff."

Blaine's whispered voice. Emotion fountained inside her, and a sob threatened to break free. She spun, burrowing into his chest. She moved, pressing her face up against the skin of his neck and breathing deep.

"You're okay?" His big hands patted her down, his sense of relief crashing over her.

"Yes. I'm fine...now."

"Good. Damn, I think you might have broken my nose."

She gave a hiccupping laugh. "Sorry. Um, it isn't bleeding. *Drak*, I am so glad you're here."

"Why? You'd already rescued yourself."

She slid her hand up and cupped his jaw, feeling the scrape of scruff on his cheek. "You came for me."

"Yes." A simple, strong word. His hand skimmed down her side and paused at her wound. He touched the stickiness at her side.

"It's nothing. Minor." Everything was fine now that Blaine was here.

She heard fabric tearing and then he was wadding cloth against her injury. "I'm sorry, baby." He cupped her cheeks and she could just see his eyes in the faint light. "I'm sorry I couldn't get you out earlier."

"It's okay. You did the right thing and took care of Winter. And you came back."

"I'll always come for you." His lips touched hers, a light flutter, then he took her mouth. The kiss deepened and she fought back a moan.

Suddenly, shouts broke out on the other side of the trading post. Saff and Blaine broke apart, and she saw the flare of light as more torches were lit.

"Dammit," Blaine bit out. "We've been discovered."

Guards were running out of a low-set building, pulling on clothes as they did. Her heart contracted. So many.

Ahead, she made out the big forms of Raiden, Galen, and Thorin racing to meet the incoming attack. The gladiators ran into the flood of guards, weapons swinging.

But there were so many enemies. Even as Harper, Nero, Lore, and Kace joined the fight, the guards kept coming. There were too many.

She spun back to Blaine, grasping at their one chance. "Now you need to embrace who you are. The fierce, violent fighter inside you."

Blaine's muscles went tense. But then he looked

past her, at their friends fighting against their enemies.

"Be the champion I know you are," she said.

He gave a nod. And then he threw his head back and gave a fierce roar that echoed around the trading post.

Blaine grabbed her hand, and they sprinted toward the fray. He stopped and snatched a sword off a body, handing it to her.

Saff liked the feel of a sword in her hand again. She spun it, focusing on the closest guards.

Beside her, Blaine raised his sword, his gaze on the enemies ahead.

Swords clashed against swords, metal rang on metal. She ran into the mass of guards, spinning and dipping. She spotted Kace, Raiden, Harper and the others. Her friends fought with the same fierce focus they used in the arena.

The fight raged. She just focused on each opponent, cutting them down.

She heard a roar and looked up to see Blaine facing the Srinar leader with the purple shirt. The man was scrambling on the ground, trying to get away from Blaine.

But Blaine never faltered. He didn't listen to the taunting words spilling from the alien's mouth. He lifted his sword, and ended his tormentor with one hard strike.

Then ahead, she saw the flicker of flames. More than just torches.

"The crud-spawn are setting the cages alight," Galen yelled.

No. There were women still locked in there.

"Fuck," Blaine snapped. "We have to help them."

Saff nodded, and they took down two more guards before circling around the fighters. Ahead of them, Galen spun into view, fighting with a powerful, mesmerizing intensity. He took down two more guards.

The flames were building, rising into the night sky. Saff heard the screams of the women caught in the cages.

They reached a wall of flames, blocking them from the cages beyond.

Blaine gripped Saff by the waist. "Trust me. I'll throw you over to the other side."

She looked at this man who had upended her neat and tidy life. She trusted him completely. She nodded.

He lifted her, swung her back, then tossed her high over the flames.

Saff flew through the air, feeling the singe on her skin as she cut through the flames, and landed, rolling through the sand. Then she was up, swinging her sword to take down the guard setting the cages alight.

She reached the closest of the burning cages and slammed her sword down on the lock. It shattered. She raced down the row, smashing lock after lock. "Go. Go!"

Women clambered out of the cages and ran. Once everyone was free, Saff skirted the wall of fire and headed back toward her friends. She saw Blaine fighting like a wild man, whirling through their opponents. He was roaring and out of control, and taking down guard after guard.

Then she turned, and saw Kace fighting a massive guard. The alien had a giant set of horns, and towered over Kace. But she knew her fight partner was a hell of a gladiator. He'd take the man.

But then she spotted another guard, sneaking up behind Kace, sword raised.

"Kace!" She raced toward her fight partner.

He was turning, but it was too late. The cowardly guard behind Kace thrust his sword into Kace's back.

Her friend's body arched backward. He hung there for a second, before the guard withdrew the blade. Kace dropped to the sand.

"No!" Saff screamed, plowing through the guards in front of her.

She needed to get to Kace. Kace, her oh-so-steady fight partner. A man who'd only just discovered love, and had a baby coming.

"Kace!"

***

Blaine took down the last guard. His chest was heaving, a red haze covering his vision.

But the bloodlust was slowly receding. He'd controlled it. He'd used his inner strength, and now he'd brought it back under control. Saff had been right.

"Kace!"

Saff's scream made Blaine spin. He saw Saff skidding to her knees beside her fallen fight partner.

Blaine sprinted toward them. As he got there, Saff was pressing her palms down on a wound on the gladiator's back. Blood was pumping out of the wound, coating her fingers.

"Drak." She pressed her hands down. "Kace."

Galen appeared and crouched beside them. The imperator cursed. "We need to get him back to Kor Magna and the healers."

"He won't make it," Blaine said. He had basic medic training, and he knew the wound was too bad. The man would bleed out long before they got back to the city.

He strode over to a downed guard and tore the man's shirt away. He wadded it up and handed it to Saff. She pressed it down on the wound.

Blaine frowned. "I have some basic skills, but this is more than I can handle."

"Winter's a healer," Nero said.

"Get her," Galen barked. Nero jogged into the darkness.

As they waited, the imperator looked around and blew out a breath. "Raiden and Harper, calm the women. Tell them they are free, and we'll arrange transport for them and get them away from here." With a nod, the couple turned to carry out his orders.

It felt like an eternity, but finally, Nero returned. Winter clung to his arm as he rushed her forward.

"What happened?" Winter asked.

"He was run through by a sword," Saff said, her voice shaky.

Blaine's jaw worked. Winter might be a doctor, but she was blind. She knelt beside Kace and reached out to touch Kace's body. "Describe what you see."

Saff started to talk, but her voice was choked. Blaine touched her shoulder and took over. "The wound looks clean, but it's bleeding badly."

Winter nodded and probed the wound with slender hands. "I think the tip of the blade has broken off inside."

Jesus. They couldn't do surgery out here.

"We need to get it out," Winter said. "Blaine, I need you to be my eyes." She lifted her head, her milky eyes turned in his direction. "Someone find something to put between his teeth. Some leather, or something."

Galen brought a piece of harness, slipping it between the gladiator's teeth.

"Ready," Blaine told her.

Winter probed the wound. The gladiator groaned.

"Easy, Kace," Saff murmured to her friend. "Let her work. You'll be okay. Rory's going to be really pissed at you for getting yourself stabbed."

Winter's face was creased as she focused. She delved her fingers into the wound, Kace groaning loudly around the harness in his teeth, and a second later, she held something up. "Got it!" She held out the tip of metal, covered in blood. "I need more fabric for a bandage. Preferably clean fabric. At least, as clean as possible out here."

The others brought her the things she needed. Soon, she was binding the wound.

Nero knelt down beside them. "I'll carry him to the transport."

Galen gave a weary nod. "The rest of you, search the freed captives for Dayna and Mia. Tell them we will head for Kor Magna and return them to their homes, or someplace safe."

Blaine grabbed Saff's hand. Her face was set in stone, and he could tell she was worried about Kace.

They moved through the group of milling women. Most were painfully thin, dirty, and bedraggled.

He scanned every face. He didn't see any humans.

"No sign of Dayna and Mia," Harper said, her voice cracking. "They aren't here."

Blaine let out a breath. Where the hell were they? He heard Raiden and some of the others questioning the women, but no one had seen anyone matching Dayna or Mia's descriptions.

"Okay," Galen said. "You're all free now. The House of Galen will ensure your safety and we'll get you back to Kor Magna. From there, you can contact your families."

Happy cries and cheers broke out. Raiden and Harper took the lead on organizing the women to take *tarnids* and transports back to the city.

Wearily, Blaine made it back to their transport.

He saw Kace's prone form laid out in the back, Saff sitting beside him.

Blaine climbed in, too, careful not to crowd her. But before he could say anything, Saff climbed on top of him, curling up in his lap. He wrapped his arms around her.

"God, I thought I'd lost you." He buried his face in her hair.

"Never," she murmured.

"Saff...you accept me as I am."

She lifted her head and smiled. "I like rough and tough." She leaned up and nipped his chin. "And you accept me as I am. Not many people have done that before."

"I like the sexy fighter, the fierce protector, and the net champion." He smiled. "The gorgeous woman and the hot lover."

She nipped him again. "Blaine."

"Let's go home," he said.

And he meant it. Home wasn't a house, a room or a place. It was wherever this woman was.

***

It was mid-morning by the time they returned to the House of Galen. Galen, Raiden, and Harper had left them to take the convoy of freed women to Varus's stables, and the imperator was planning to call in Rillian to help get them home.

Blaine climbed off the transport just outside the Kor Magna Arena, helping Saff off with him. She was moving stiffly and he wanted her side looked at as soon as possible. They'd dozed as best they could on the journey back, but damn he was tired.

He grabbed her arm, bringing her branded wrist up to his lips for a quick kiss. "First thing, we get rid of this."

She smiled and leaned into him. Tugging her close, he looked up at the stone walls of the arena. His home. For the first time since his abduction, he felt something settle inside him.

Blaine still felt the emotions inside him and he knew his control would never be the same, but he could be a damn good gladiator of the House of Galen, and still help people. He looked down at Saff's dark head. And with Saff by his side— fighting with him, challenging him, loving him— his new life would be damn near perfect.

He heard shouts and watched as Regan, Rory, and Madeline exploded out of a doorway from the arena.

"Thank God." Rory threw her arms around Blaine and then Saff.

Regan smiled at them. "We are so glad you guys are back."

Rory's gaze narrowed and she grinned. "You guys did the nasty." She held out a palm to the others. "I win."

Madeline shook her head. "I thought for sure you'd wait until you got back." She slapped a coin in Rory's palm.

Blaine cleared his throat. "Rory?"

His tone of voice must have warned her. Her hand flew to cover her belly protectively and her gaze scanned their group. "Where's Kace?"

"He was hurt—"

"No." She raced to the transport, just as Thorin hefted the wounded gladiator out.

"Rory." Saff wrapped an arm around the woman. "He's alive. You need to stay calm so you don't disturb him. We need to get him to Medical."

Rory nodded, tears in her eyes. "He'll be fine. He's tough." She hurried along beside her lover, Regan going with her.

Madeline's gaze was tracking Lore as the man helped Winter down from Nero's *tarnid*. She glanced at Blaine. "You found Winter."

"Yeah. She's rattled, but she's fine."

"Dayna? Mia?"

He shook his head.

Pain spasmed on Madeline's face. "God, where are they?"

Worse, what were they being subjected to? Blaine squeezed Madeline's shoulder. "We aren't giving up."

Madeline nodded and a second later, Lore appeared, sweeping her into his arms. With Nero clutching Winter, they moved inside.

Blaine released a breath. "I need a hot shower and a nap."

Saff grinned at him. "No stamina."

"Excuse me? I think you've forgotten what we did the other night."

She pressed into him, lowering her voice. "I haven't forgotten."

Memories peppered him and he groaned. "Well, I

guess it's time I show you what I can do in a shower."

Interest sparked in her dark eyes. "Sounds good to me, Earth man. Very good."

He slung an arm across her shoulders, leading her inside. "Then I'm going to cook for you. Galen probably has some sort of grill around here."

"I have something planned for you, too." Her voice was almost a purr.

The sound made Blaine's cock hard. "Oh?"

She turned to face him, walking backward. "I promised to get down on my knees and pleasure you." She licked her lips. "But only if you're interested." With that, she turned and strode into the House of Galen.

Blaine stared after her. Yep, perfect.

He hurried after her.

***

Saff had a bounce in her step as she entered her bedroom.

Instantly, she saw Blaine's clothes mixed with hers over the back of a chair. She spotted the chunky comp screen she'd gotten for him on the bedside table.

Not her room, *their* room.

She smiled to herself. Happy. She was so drakking happy.

They'd returned from the desert three days ago. Thanks to Winter, Kace had survived the journey. He'd spent an hour in a regen tank, with Rory by his side, and was now fully healed. He'd been complaining about Hero. Apparently, the dog wanted to sleep by Kace's side and kept bringing him small gifts—usually dead rodents.

Galen had told them that all the women had made it back to Kor Magna. Many had already been reunited with their families.

Her pulse skipped. The only blot on their happiness was the fact that they hadn't found Dayna and Mia. Not even a whisper about the women.

But they hadn't given up looking, and they never would.

Saff strode across the room to the window, where the gauzy curtains were dancing in the wind. Below, she saw Nero and Lore leading new recruits through training exercises in the training arena. She was on shift later with Blaine, and then Duna was due tonight to come and watch the House of Galen in the arena. The girl had sent Saff several messages to ensure she hadn't forgotten.

Saff glanced in the direction of Medical. There was no sign of the damage that had been done by the explosion. Galen had ensured the repairs were made swiftly. She also knew he was working on upgraded security, even working with Zhim to install some high-tech system.

More than that, she knew Galen was working hard on a plan to find Zaabha and end the Srinar and the House of Thrax once and for all.

She'd made a good life for herself here at the House of Galen, but it had taken Blaine to make her realize that she'd been skimming through her life. Because of the hurts of her past, she'd not allowed herself to form any deeper romantic attachments.

But then again, maybe it was because she'd never met the right man before Blaine.

Here she was, in love. Her grin widened. Saff Essikani was in love with a sexy man from the other side of the galaxy.

She moved back toward the bed. Maybe she'd take a shower before—

The attack came suddenly.

A weight barreled into her from behind, and she was forced across the room and shoved facefirst onto the bed.

She jerked backward, fighting for her freedom. But her opponent was far heavier than she was.

"You have nowhere to go, gladiator," the deep voice breathed in her ear. Hot breath brushed over the side of her neck. "You're all mine, now."

Desire ignited, pooling low in her belly, as Blaine dominated her. He pushed her harder into the bed. She loved the feel of his big body on hers.

"That's what you think." She bucked hard, and they rolled across the bed. They tussled, and, for a second, she looked up at his rough, rugged face— his beloved face—and he was smiling. Wide, open, and free. He'd been smiling more these last few days since they'd returned from the desert.

She leaned up and kissed him, then she bit down on his lip, tasting blood.

He reared his head back. "Bloodthirsty."

She laughed. "And don't you forget it."

He used all his strength to flip her, until she was facedown in the pillows. She wrestled, fighting him, but he pinned her. Then her tight trousers were torn off her body.

And a second later, the thick, mushroom head of his cock probed her thighs. She groaned.

"Feel that?" he said on a growl. "It's going to fill you up."

Drak, yes. He thrust deep.

Saff moaned, arching and pushing back against him. He filled her so well, stretching her beyond what she thought possible. Her hands twisted in the covers as he powered into her.

Soon, the room was filled with their mingled groans, and the slap of flesh.

"I'm going to come, Blaine." She was shifting wildly against him.

"Yes. Let it come. Cry my name."

She did. Her orgasm crashed over her, and it was Blaine's name torn from her lips. A second later, he thrust once and poured himself inside her.

They both dropped down on their bed, shattered. Time passed, and Blaine toyed idly with her hair.

"We still haven't found Dayna and Mia," she said.

"No. But we won't give up. We'll find them, no matter how long it takes."

That was her fierce champion. A man who never gave up, despite the odds.

"I love you," he murmured, nuzzling her head.

Her heart swelled. Her mother had talked of

love, but she couldn't have known what the real thing felt like.

Now Saff did. She felt the bright, hot, and sweet emotion engulfing her. "I love you, too."

She saw a flash in his eyes. "I don't want to own you, Saff, but I want you to be mine."

"As long as you're mine, too." She moved her hands over his bare chest, her fingers tracing over his smooth skin. He'd had most of his scars healed just yesterday, but there were a few faint traces here and there. A badge of honor that he'd survived and come out the other side. "As long as you let me love all of you. The wild man inside you, too."

He nodded. "I came across the galaxy to find you, Saff."

Heart melting, she rolled on top of him. "Then let me show you just how much I appreciate that, Earth man."

"First one to make the other orgasm wins," he murmured, his hands cupping her breasts.

She laughed. "How about the best of three?"

I hope you enjoyed Saff and Blaine's story! Galactic Gladiators continues with BARBARIAN, starring barbarian gladiator Nero, coming mid-2017. For more action-packed romance, read on for a preview of the first chapter of *Marcus*, the first book in my bestselling Hell Squad series.

Don't miss out! For updates about new releases, action romance info, free books, and other fun stuff, sign up for my VIP mailing list and get your *free box set* containing three action-packed romances.

Visit here to get started:
www.annahackettbooks.com

FREE BOX SET DOWNLOAD

JOIN THE ACTION-PACKED ADVENTURE!

Formats: Kindle, ePub, PDF

Preview – Hell Squad: Marcus

READY FOR ANOTHER?

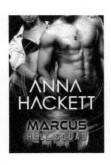

IN THE AFTERMATH OF AN ALIEN INVASION:

**HEROES WILL RISE...
WHEN THEY HAVE
SOMEONE TO LIVE FOR**

Her team was under attack.

Elle Milton pressed her fingers to her small earpiece. "Squad Six, you have seven more raptors inbound from the east." Her other hand gripped the edge of her comp screen, showing the enhanced drone feed.

She watched, her belly tight, as seven glowing red dots converged on the blue ones huddled together in the burned-out ruin of an office building in downtown Sydney. Each blue dot was a squad member and one of them was their leader.

"Marcus? Do you copy?" Elle fought to keep her voice calm. No way she'd let them hear her alarm.

"Roger that, Elle." Marcus' gravelly voice filled her ear. Along with the roar of laser fire. "We see them."

She sagged back in her chair. This was the worst part. Just sitting there knowing that Marcus and the others were fighting for their lives. In the six months she'd been comms officer for the squad, she'd worked hard to learn the ropes. But there were days she wished she was out there, aiming a gun and taking out as many alien raptors as she could.

You're not a soldier, Ellianna. No, she was a useless party-girl-turned-survivor. She watched as a red dot disappeared off the screen, then another, and another. She finally drew a breath. Marcus and his team were the experienced soldiers. She'd just be a big fat liability in the field.

But she was a damn good comms officer.

Just then, a new cluster of red dots appeared near the team. She tapped the screen, took a measurement. "Marcus! More raptors are en route. They're about one kilometer away. North." God, would these invading aliens ever leave them alone?

"Shit," Marcus bit out. Then he went silent.

She didn't know if he was thinking or fighting. She pictured his rugged, scarred face creased in thought as he formulated a plan.

Then his deep, rasping voice was back. "Elle, we need an escape route and an evac now. Shaw's been hit in the leg, Cruz is carrying him. We can't engage more raptors."

She tapped the screen rapidly, pulling up drone images and archived maps. *Escape route, escape route.* Her mind clicked through the options. She knew Shaw was taller and heavier than Cruz, but the armor they wore had slim-line exoskeletons built into them allowing the soldiers to lift heavier loads and run faster and longer than normal. She tapped the screen again. *Come on.* She needed somewhere safe for a Hawk quadcopter to set down and pick them up.

"Elle? We need it now!"

Just then her comp beeped. She looked at the image and saw a hazy patch of red appear in the broken shell of a nearby building. The heat sensor had detected something else down there. Something big.

Right next to the team.

She touched her ear. "Rex! Marcus, a rex has just woken up in the building beside you."

"Fuck! Get us out of here. Now."

Oh, God. Elle swallowed back bile. Images of rexes, with their huge, dinosaur-like bodies and mouths full of teeth, flashed in her head.

More laser fire ripped through her earpiece and she heard the wild roar of the awakening beast.

Block it out. She focused on the screen. Marcus needed her. The team needed her.

"Run past the rex." One hand curled into a tight fist, her nails cutting into her skin. "Go through its hiding place."

"Through its nest?" Marcus' voice was incredulous. "You know how territorial they are."

"It's the best way out. On the other side you'll find a railway tunnel. Head south along it about eight hundred meters, and you'll find an emergency exit ladder that you can take to the surface. I'll have a Hawk pick you up there."

A harsh expulsion of breath. "Okay, Elle. You've gotten us out of too many tight spots for me to doubt you now."

His words had heat creeping into her cheeks. His praise...it left her giddy. In her life BAI—before alien invasion—no one had valued her opinions. Her father, her mother, even her almost-fiancé, they'd all thought her nothing more than a pretty ornament. Hell, she *had* been a silly, pretty party girl.

And because she'd been inept, her parents were dead. Elle swallowed. A year had passed since that horrible night during the first wave of the alien attack, when their giant ships had appeared in the skies. Her parents had died that night, along with most of the world.

"Hell Squad, ready to go to hell?" Marcus called out.

"Hell, yeah!" the team responded. "The devil needs an ass-kicking!"

"Woo-hoo!" Another voice blasted through her headset, pulling her from the past. "Ellie, baby, this dirty alien's nest stinks like Cruz's socks. You should be here."

A smile tugged at Elle's lips. Shaw Baird always

knew how to ease the tension of a life-or-death situation.

"Oh, yeah, Hell Squad gets the best missions," Shaw added.

Elle watched the screen, her smile slipping. Everyone called Squad Six the Hell Squad. She was never quite sure if it was because they were hellions, or because they got sent into hell to do the toughest, dirtiest missions.

There was no doubt they were a bunch of rebels. Marcus had a rep for not following orders. Just the previous week, he'd led the squad in to destroy a raptor outpost but had detoured to rescue survivors huddled in an abandoned hospital that was under attack. At the debrief, the general's yelling had echoed through the entire base. Marcus, as always, had been silent.

"Shut up, Shaw, you moron." The deep female voice carried an edge.

Elle had decided there were two words that best described the only female soldier on Hell Squad— loner and tough. Claudia Frost was everything Elle wasn't. Elle cleared her throat. "Just get yourselves back to base."

As she listened to the team fight their way through the rex nest, she tapped in the command for one of the Hawk quadcopters to pick them up.

The line crackled. "Okay, Elle, we're through. Heading to the evac point."

Marcus' deep voice flowed over her and the tense muscles in her shoulders relaxed a fraction. They'd be back soon. They were okay. He was okay.

She pressed a finger to the blue dot leading the team. "The bird's en route, Marcus."

"Thanks. See you soon."

She watched on the screen as the large, black shadow of the Hawk hovered above the ground and the team boarded. The rex was headed in their direction, but they were already in the air.

Elle stood and ran her hands down her trousers. She shot a wry smile at the camouflage fabric. It felt like a dream to think that she'd ever owned a very expensive, designer wardrobe. And heels—God, how long had it been since she'd worn heels? These days, fatigues were all that hung in her closet. Well-worn ones, at that.

As she headed through the tunnels of the underground base toward the landing pads, she forced herself not to run. She'd see him—them—soon enough. She rounded a corner and almost collided with someone.

"General. Sorry, I wasn't watching where I was going."

"No problem, Elle." General Adam Holmes had a military-straight bearing he'd developed in the United Coalition Army and a head of dark hair with a brush of distinguished gray at his temples. He was classically handsome, and his eyes were a piercing blue. He was the top man in this last little outpost of humanity. "Squad Six on their way back?"

"Yes, sir." They fell into step.

"And they secured the map?"

God, Elle had almost forgotten about the map.

"Ah, yes. They got images of it just before they came under attack by raptors."

"Well, let's go welcome them home. That map might just be the key to the fate of mankind."

They stepped into the landing areas. Staff in various military uniforms and civilian clothes raced around. After the raptors had attacked, bringing all manner of vicious creatures with them to take over the Earth, what was left of mankind had banded together.

Whoever had survived now lived here in an underground base in the Blue Mountains, just west of Sydney, or in the other, similar outposts scattered across the planet. All arms of the United Coalition's military had been decimated. In the early days, many of the surviving soldiers had fought amongst themselves, trying to work out who outranked whom. But it didn't take long before General Holmes had unified everyone against the aliens. Most squads were a mix of ranks and experience, but the teams eventually worked themselves out. Most didn't even bother with titles and rank anymore.

Sirens blared, followed by the clang of metal. Huge doors overhead retracted into the roof.

A Hawk filled the opening, with its sleek gray body and four spinning rotors. It was near-silent, running on a small thermonuclear engine. It turned slowly as it descended to the landing pad.

Her team was home.

She threaded her hands together, her heart beating a little faster.

Marcus was home.

Marcus Steele wanted a shower and a beer.

Hot, sweaty and covered in raptor blood, he leaped down from the Hawk and waved at his team to follow. He kept a sharp eye on the medical team who raced out to tend to Shaw. Dr. Emerson Green was leading them, her white lab coat snapping around her curvy body. The blonde doctor caught his gaze and tossed him a salute.

Shaw was cursing and waving them off, but one look from Marcus and the lanky Australian sniper shut his mouth.

Marcus swung his laser carbine over his shoulder and scraped a hand down his face. Man, he'd kill for a hot shower. Of course, he'd have to settle for a cold one since they only allowed hot water for two hours in the morning in order to conserve energy. But maybe after that beer he'd feel human again.

"Well done, Squad Six." Holmes stepped forward. "Steele, I hear you got images of the map."

Holmes might piss Marcus off sometimes, but at least the guy always got straight to the point. He was a general to the bone and always looked spit and polish. Everything about him screamed money and a fancy education, so not surprisingly, he tended to rub the troops the wrong way.

Marcus pulled the small, clear comp chip from his pocket. "We got it."

Then he spotted her.

Shit. It was always a small kick in his chest. His gaze traveled up Elle Milton's slim figure, coming to rest on a face he could stare at all day. She wasn't very tall, but that didn't matter. Something about her high cheekbones, pale-blue eyes, full lips, and rain of chocolate-brown hair...it all worked for him. Perfectly. She was beautiful, kind, and far too good to be stuck in this crappy underground maze of tunnels, dressed in hand-me-down fatigues.

She raised a slim hand. Marcus shot her a small nod.

"Hey, Ellie-girl. Gonna give me a kiss?"

Shaw passed on an iono-stretcher hovering off the ground and Marcus gritted his teeth. The tall, blond sniper with his lazy charm and Aussie drawl was popular with the ladies. Shaw flashed his killer smile at Elle.

She smiled back, her blue eyes twinkling and Marcus' gut cramped.

Then she put one hand on her hip and gave the sniper a head-to-toe look. She shook her head. "I think you get enough kisses."

Marcus released the breath he didn't realize he was holding.

"See you later, Sarge." Zeke Jackson slapped Marcus on the back and strolled past. His usually-silent twin, Gabe, was beside him. The twins, both former Coalition Army Special Forces soldiers, were deadly in the field. Marcus was damned happy to have them on his squad.

"Howdy, Princess." Claudia shot Elle a smirk as

she passed.

Elle rolled her eyes. "Claudia."

Cruz, Marcus' second-in-command and best friend from their days as Coalition Marines, stepped up beside Marcus and crossed his arms over his chest. He'd already pulled some of his lightweight body armor off, and the ink on his arms was on display.

The general nodded at Cruz before looking back at Marcus. "We need Shaw back up and running ASAP. If the raptor prisoner we interrogated is correct, that map shows one of the main raptor communications hubs." There was a blaze of excitement in the usually-stoic general's voice. "It links all their operations together."

Yeah, Marcus knew it was big. Destroy the hub, send the raptor operations into disarray.

The general continued. "As soon as the tech team can break the encryption on the chip and give us a location for the raptor comms hub—" his piercing gaze leveled on Marcus "—I want your team back out there to plant the bomb."

Marcus nodded. He knew if they destroyed the raptors' communications it gave humanity a fighting chance. A chance they desperately needed.

He traded a look with Cruz. Looked like they were going out to wade through raptor gore again sooner than anticipated.

Man, he really wanted that beer.

Then Marcus' gaze landed on Elle again. He didn't keep going out there for himself, or Holmes. He went so people like Elle and the other civilian survivors had a chance. A chance to do more than simply survive.

"Shaw's wound is minor. Doc Emerson should have him good as new in an hour or so." Since the advent of the nano-meds, simple wounds could be healed in hours, rather than days and weeks. They carried a dose of the microscopic medical machines on every mission, but only for dire emergencies. The nano-meds had to be administered and monitored by professionals or they were just as likely to kill you from the inside than heal you.

General Holmes nodded. "Good."

Elle cleared her throat. "There's no telling how long it will take to break the encryption. I've been working with the tech team and even if they break it, we may not be able to translate it all. We're getting better at learning the raptor language but there are still huge amounts of it we don't yet understand."

Marcus' jaw tightened. There was always something. He knew Noah Kim—their resident genius computer specialist—and his geeks were good, but if they couldn't read the damn raptor language...

Holmes turned. "Steele, let your team have some downtime and be ready the minute Noah has anything."

"Yes, sir." As the general left, Marcus turned to Cruz. "Go get yourself a beer, Ramos."

"Don't need to tell me more than once, *amigo*. I would kill for some of my dad's tamales to go with it." Something sad flashed across a face all the women in the base mooned over, then he grimaced and a bone-deep weariness colored his words. "Need to wash the raptor off me, first." He tossed Marcus a casual salute, Elle a smile, and strode out.

Marcus frowned after his friend and absently started loosening his body armor.

Elle moved up beside him. "I can take the comp chip to Noah."

"Sure." He handed it to her. When her fingers brushed his he felt the warmth all the way through him. Hell, he had it bad. Thankfully, he still had his armor on or she'd see his cock tenting his pants.

"I'll come find you as soon as we have something." She glanced up at him. Smiled. "Are you going to rec night tonight? I hear Cruz might even play guitar for us."

The Friday-night gathering was a chance for everyone to blow off a bit of steam and drink too much homebrewed beer. And Cruz had an unreal talent with a guitar, although lately Marcus hadn't seen the man play too much.

Marcus usually made an appearance at these parties, then left early to head back to his room to study raptor movements or plan the squad's next missions. "Yeah, I'll be there."

"Great." She smiled. "I'll see you there, then." She hurried out clutching the chip.

He stared at the tunnel where she'd exited for a long while after she disappeared, and finally ripped his chest armor off. Ah, on second thought, maybe going to the rec night wasn't a great idea. Watching her pretty face and captivating smile would drive him crazy. He cursed under his breath. He really needed that cold shower.

As he left the landing pads, he reminded himself he should be thinking of the mission. Destroy the hub and kill more aliens. Rinse and repeat. Death and killing, that was about all he knew.

He breathed in and caught a faint trace of Elle's floral scent. She was clean and fresh and good. She always worried about them, always had a smile, and she was damned good at providing their comms and intel.

She was why he fought through the muck every day. So she could live and the goodness in her would survive. She deserved more than blood and death and killing.

And she sure as hell deserved more than a battled-scarred, bloodstained soldier.

Hell Squad

Marcus

Cruz

Gabe

Reed

Roth

Noah

Shaw

Holmes

Niko

Finn

Devlin

Also by Anna Hackett

Treasure Hunter Security
Undiscovered
Uncharted
Unexplored
Unfathomed

Galactic Gladiators
Gladiator
Warrior
Hero
Protector
Champion

Hell Squad
Marcus
Cruz
Gabe
Reed
Roth
Noah
Shaw
Holmes
Niko
Finn
Devlin

The Anomaly Series
Time Thief
Mind Raider
Soul Stealer
Salvation
Anomaly Series Box Set

The Phoenix Adventures
Among Galactic Ruins
At Star's End
In the Devil's Nebula
On a Rogue Planet
Beneath a Trojan Moon
Beyond Galaxy's Edge
On a Cyborg Planet
Return to Dark Earth
On a Barbarian World
Lost in Barbarian Space
Through Uncharted Space

Perma Series
Winter Fusion

The WindKeepers Series
Wind Kissed, Fire Bound
Taken by the South Wind
Tempting the West Wind
Defying the North Wind
Claiming the East Wind

Standalone Titles
Savage Dragon
Hunter's Surrender
One Night with the Wolf

Anthologies
A Galactic Holiday
Moonlight (UK only)
Vampire Hunter (UK only)
Awakening the Dragon (UK Only)

For more information visit AnnaHackettBooks.com

About the Author

I'm a USA Today bestselling author and I'm passionate about *action romance*. I love stories that combine the thrill of falling in love with the excitement of action, danger and adventure. I'm a sucker for that moment when the team is walking in slow motion, shoulder-to-shoulder heading off into battle.

I write about people overcoming unbeatable odds and achieving seemingly impossible goals. I like to believe it's possible for all of us to do the same.

My books are mixture of action, adventure and sexy romance and they're recommended for anyone who enjoys fast-paced stories where the boy wins the girl at the end (or sometimes the girl wins the boy!)

For release dates, action romance info, free books, and other fun stuff, sign up for the latest news here:

Website: AnnaHackettBooks.com

Lightning Source UK Ltd.
Milton Keynes UK
UKHW041815170219
337497UK00001B/9/P